W9-AMQ-172

Shadow Horse

by
Alison Hart

Shadow Horse

by

Alison Hart

RANDOM HOUSE NEW YORK

www.randomhouse.com/kids

Library of Congress Cataloging-in-Publication Data
Hart, Alison.
Shadow Horse / by Alison Hart
p.   cm.
Summary: Thirteen-year-old Jas tries to prove that the owner of the farm
where she works has killed her favorite horse, Whirlwind.
ISBN: 0-679-88642-7
[1. Horses–Fiction. 2. Animals–Treatment–Fiction. 3. Mystery and detective
stories.] I. Title.
PZ7.H256272Sh   1999
[Fic]–dc21

98-43845

Printed in the United States of America   10 9 8 7 6 5 4 3 2 1

Acknowledgments

To the dedicated professionals who shared their time and knowledge: Susan Weisgerber, juvenile case manager at Staunton-Augusta Court Service Unit; Rod Jones, probation supervisor at 25th District Juvenile and Domestic Relations Court Service Unit; Corporal Tom Byerly of the Staunton Police Department; Dana Wandless, social worker at Staunton-Augusta Department of Social Services.

Special thanks to Patricia Rogers, Manager of the Equine Rescue League in Leesburg, Virginia. Your energy and enthusiasm were inspirational.

Chapter 1

She was a flash of gold as she cantered around the ring. Ears pricked, neck arched, she moved like a movie star in the spotlight as she sailed over the last fence. Landing smoothly, she slowed to a trot in front of the crowd, tossing her mane as if to say, "Wasn't I great?"

Because she *was* great. She was the most beautiful horse in the world.

But now she was dead.

Whirlwind.

Jas whispered the mare's name as she stared at the photo clutched in her fingers. Whirlwind was posed for the camera with her head high, a tricolored ribbon fluttering from her bridle. The picture had been taken a month ago at Devon, the horse show where they'd won the Junior Hunter Championship.

Now this picture was all Jas had left of the mare she loved.

Tears welled in her eyes. She hadn't cried since the chestnut horse died three weeks ago. She wasn't about to now.

Clapping her hand over her mouth, Jas tried to hold back a sob. The paper grocery bag on her lap slid sideways. She grabbed for it, but the handcuffs bit into her wrists, and the bag fell, spilling her underwear onto the floor of the Municipal Court holding room.

Someone in the room snickered. Flushing hotly, Jas bent over and scooped her underwear back into the bag.

The kid sitting next to her leaned closer. "Hey, can I have those?" he whispered.

"No," Jas retorted, shrinking from his leering face. "They're all the clothes I've got." Sitting up, she crumpled the bag to her chest.

A silent cry filled her.

Grandfather!

If only he was here. Jas knew if he was, none of this would be happening. She'd be schooling a horse at High Meadows Farm and not waiting for the court bailiff to call her name.

"Move to another seat, Vince," a deputy barked at the kid sitting next to Jas.

From the corner of her eye, Jas watched Vince swagger across the floor, his defiant gaze directed at the two deputies standing guard. The deputies wore tan suit coats with the sheriff's department emblem over the pocket. One stood in an army stance. The other sat on a folding chair with his long legs stretched in front of him. The rest of the holding room was filled with teenagers.

Jas was the only girl.

Turning away, Jas stared out the barred window that overlooked Stanford's Main Street. A man wearing a dark suit walked briskly down the sidewalk, a soft breeze ruffling his hair.

"Jasmine?"

She snapped her head around. Charles Petrie, the public defender, looked down at her with his half-glasses perched on his nose.

"We'll be called sometime in the next hour," Petrie said. "Unfortunately, there's no set schedule." Impatiently, he ran his fingers through his thinning hair. "Is there anything you want to tell me before we see the judge?" He sat down next to her, balancing his briefcase on his knees.

Jas shook her head.

He let out an exasperated sigh. It was the same sigh Jas had heard the last time he'd asked that question.

"I can't help you if you won't tell me what happened." He waited. Jas didn't say anything. He exhaled loudly, expressing his annoyance. "Okay.

I'm going to defend you, but I don't know how well we're going to do."

He stood up. "I'll see you in court. If you change your mind, tell one of the deputies to come get me."

"I won't change my mind," Jas replied. She *couldn't* change her mind.

"Hey, beautiful," Vince said as he sat down in Petrie's vacant chair. He was about her age, thirteen, or maybe older.

"Beautiful?" Jas said as she wrinkled her nose. She'd barely slept or eaten for three weeks. Her tan had faded. Her once well-muscled arms and legs were soft from inactivity. Her brown hair had been washed only once since she'd been put in the detention center by the judge at the first hearing.

The first hearing—she could still remember everything the judge had said: *Jasmine Schuler, you have been charged with a felony. Since there is no one to release you to at this time, you will be held in the Juvenile Detention Center until your trial on June fifteenth.*

That had been fourteen days ago. It seemed like a lifetime.

"You're definitely the most beautiful babe in here," Vince said.

Jas rolled her eyes. "I'm the *only* girl in here."

"Yeah, I noticed." He tossed his hair off his brow with a shrug of his head. "What're you here for?"

"Same reason you're here. The cops caught me," which was the same line Jas told any kid who asked. Not that many at the center had asked anyway. They were too busy with their own problems.

"Yeah? Were you busted for drugs, too?"

"No, just a runaway," Jas lied.

"Been there, too. This time, the cops caught me with marijuana." He jabbed his thumb at his skinny chest as if he was proud of it.

Jas gave him her best get-lost look. Maybe if she told him why she was *really* here he would shut up.

She turned her back to him and glanced around the room. It was full of guys just like the punk sitting next to her. They were talking and laughing as if they were waiting for homeroom to begin, instead of court. Only one skinny kid looked scared. He was slumped in a corner, his eyes downcast. His mother was huddled just as miserably next to him.

At least he has someone, Jas thought. She crossed her fingers, hoping that Phil Sparks, the manager of High Meadows, would come to the trial. Phil was her only chance. He could make the judge understand.

"Schuler case!" The words rang down the hall, and Jas jumped. The deputy leaning against the wall came over. "Ready?" he asked as he bent down to take off her handcuffs.

Jas's stomach rolled. *No, I'm not!*

"Let's go." He took the bag from her, then grasped her arm almost politely. Jas stood on shaky legs. She tried to swallow, but her mouth was too dry.

"Bye, beautiful!" Vince called, making kissing noises as the deputy led her out the door. "Clear the hall!" yelled the bailiff.

The deputy steered Jas through a group of people and into the courtroom. In the front of the room, a robed judge sat at his desk. Charles Petrie stood behind the defense table to the right of the desk, facing the judge. Mr. Eyler, the probation officer, sat against the wall. Hugh Robicheaux sat at the prosecutor's table on the left.

Jas froze when she saw Hugh. Anger rose in her chest. When she began to walk down the aisle again, her eyes bore into the back of Hugh's head. He was talking to his lawyer, a man in a dark suit, Mr. Sydow. As she looked at Hugh, she realized that she'd never hated anyone so much in her life.

"Jas?" someone called in a low voice.

Startled, Jas glanced back. Phil Sparks sat in an aisle seat behind Hugh, nervously twisting his John Deere cap in his work-roughened hands.

Phil! Jas smiled hopefully. But the farm manager ducked his head as if embarrassed. When he wouldn't meet Jas's eyes, her smile died. *Please, Phil, don't let Hugh scare you into not helping me!* With a firm grip, the deputy propelled her up the aisle to the seat next to Mr. Petrie. Jas's knees buckled, and she sat down with a thump on the wooden chair.

"Jasmine Schuler, please stand," the judge's voice rang through the courtroom.

Slowly, Jas stood, her hands clenched in fists.

"Miss Schuler, you have been charged with assault against Hugh Robicheaux."

As she heard the judge's words, Jas trembled. Again she had to fight back tears. If Phil was testifying for Hugh, she didn't stand a chance.

Hugh Robicheaux would win again.

Chapter 2

"Mr. Petrie." The judge directed his gaze at Jas. "How does your client plead?"

Jas caught her breath.

"Your honor, Miss Schuler pleads not guilty," Petrie said.

"You may be seated. Mr. Sydow, call your first witness."

Mr. Sydow, the man in the dark suit, stood up. "I'd like to call Officer Tom Diamond." Jas slumped into her seat as a Stanford police officer walked to the front and sat in the witness box.

"Officer Diamond," Mr. Sydow began, "were you called to High Meadows Farm on the night of June first?"

"I was."

"Will you please summarize the facts and circumstances at the farm on this date?"

Jas looked down at the ground as she remembered that horrible day.

Grandfather! Come quick! It's Whirlwind!

I think she's dead!

"I arrived at the farm at five in the afternoon to find the defendant, Miss Schuler, kneeling by her grandfather outside the barn," the officer said. "The rescue squad arrived minutes before, and the EMTs were treating him. They pointed to the barn, where I found the victim, Mr. Robicheaux, being attended to for a slash on his cheek."

"And what did the victim tell you?"

"He said the defendant had attacked him with a hoof pick."

"A hoof pick," Mr. Sydow repeated. The judge furrowed his brow. The attorney approached the bench carrying a manila envelope. "Your Honor, a hoof pick is a sharp tool used for cleaning out a horse's foot."

Hoof, you blockhead, Jas thought to herself.

"And is this the hoof pick you recovered, Officer Diamond?" The attorney pulled the hooked instrument out of the envelope and held it up.

"Yes."

"Thank you. You may cross-examine the witness, Mr. Petrie."

Petrie stood up, his chair scraping on the tile floor. "Officer Diamond, did you see my client attack the victim?"

"No."

"Was she at all combative when you arrived?"

"No."

"Did she give you a hard time when you arrested her?"

The officer paused. Jas held her breath. "At first, she was reluctant to leave her grandfather. The medical technicians were still working on him, and she wanted to make sure he was okay. But when I told her I would call the hospital as soon as we reached the police station, she came willingly."

"No further questions." Petrie sat down.

"Call the next witness," the judge stated.

"Mr. Hugh Robicheaux," Mr. Sydow said.

Goose bumps raced up Jas's arms as Hugh strode to the witness box and settled his long frame in the chair. He was dressed in creased khaki pants and a tweed sport coat. A thin purplish scar ran down his left cheek, marring his handsome country-gentleman demeanor.

"Mr. Robicheaux, you are the owner of High Meadows Farm?" Mr. Sydow asked.

"I am."

"And the defendant, Jasmine Schuler, and her grandfather, Karl Schuler, lived on your farm?"

"Yes, for the past five years Karl Schuler was the farm's caretaker. And when his granddaughter, Jas, wasn't in school, she would work for me as well. Jas's grandmother also lived on the farm, until she died a year ago. She acted as my house-keeper."

"And what type of work did Jasmine Schuler do at the farm?"

"Mostly she schooled and showed my horses. She was an excellent equestrienne."

Tilting his head, Hugh smiled at Jas. She glared back, knowing how false his smile was and how easily he could pour on the charm.

"Mr. Robicheaux, please tell us what happened the afternoon of June first."

"The incident started when Jas found one of my horses dead in the paddock. The mare had eaten a branch of yew, which is highly poisonous."

Jas squeezed her eyes shut tight, trying not to remember the pain of that day. But it was too hard to forget. *How did the yew get in here? Karl? Do you have an explanation for this?*

No, Mr. Robicheaux. I know how poisonous yew is. You know I would never be so careless.

But you were the only one trimming the hedges!

Sir, you can't accuse me of killing Whirlwind. You know that I'm not capable of such a thing!

Who else could have done it?

Sir, it wasn't–ahhgrh!

Grandfather, wh-what's wrong? Grandfather!

Jas shuddered. Clenching her fists, she dug her fingernails into her palms. She hadn't seen her grandfather since the day he collapsed. Now he was in a nursing home, his muscles partially paralyzed by a stroke. And she couldn't help but blame Hugh Robicheaux for this whole mess.

"Thank you, Mr. Robicheaux. Mr. Petrie, you may cross-examine the witness."

Jas's lawyer stood up. "Mr. Robicheaux, why do you think Miss Schuler attacked you?"

Jas straightened in her chair, staring intently at Hugh.

With a pensive frown, Hugh ran his fingers through his thick, carefully styled hair, then shook his head. "I don't know. I suppose she was distraught because her grandfather caused the death of her favorite horse–accidentally, of course," he added quickly.

Liar, Jas hissed to herself.

"Then her grandfather collapsed right in front of her," Hugh continued. Pausing, as if in thought, he made a steeple of his fingers. "I realize now that she was probably in shock. I should have been more understanding."

"So you said or did nothing to provoke her?"

"No."

Dirty, fat liar. Crossing her arms, Jas threw herself against the back of the chair.

"I have no further questions, Your Honor," Petrie said as he sat down.

Mr. Sydow stood up. "We call Phil Sparks to the stand."

Hat in hand, the farm manager trudged to the witness box and sat on the edge of the chair. Eyes straight ahead, he rigidly faced the attorney, as if afraid to look at Jas.

"Mr. Sparks, you are the manager of High Meadows Farm?"

"Yes, sir."

"And what are your duties on the farm?"

"I make sure it runs smoothly. Mr. Robicheaux owns over twenty horses and a hundred head of cattle, so I'm kept pretty busy."

"Will you please tell the court what happened the evening of June first."

Phil swallowed hard. He glanced once at Jas, with a pleading look in his eyes. Jas bit her lip, wishing she could tell him it was okay to tell the truth.

"I was in the driveway on the other side of the barn when I heard Jas scream," Phil said.

"You knew it was her?"

"Yes, sir. I ran around the corner and saw her attack Mr. Robicheaux."

"With the hoof pick?"

"Yes. She slashed his cheek. I ran up and pulled her off him."

"So you saw her attack him." The attorney turned and gave Jas an appraising look. "And what was she like when you pulled her off?"

"She—" Phil hesitated. Jas could see his Adam's apple rise and fall. "She was kicking and screaming."

"When did she calm down?"

"After Mr. Robicheaux told me he was going to the tack room to get something for his face. His cheek was bleeding pretty good. When he left, she pulled free and went to her grandfather, who was lying on the ground. I ran in the house to call 911."

Jas pressed her lips together, remembering what had happened when Phil left to call 911. Hugh had stormed back in and, grabbing her arm, yanked her to her feet.

You better keep quiet, Jas.

Let go of me!

One mention of your crazy suspicion that I killed Whirlwind, and I'll make sure your grandfather ends up in some rat-infested nursing home. Forever. Then I'll make sure you never see him again. But keep your mouth shut, and he'll get the best of care. Is it a deal?

You're hurting me!

Say it's a deal or I'll rip your arm off!

Okay, it's a deal!

"Thank you, Mr. Sparks," said Mr. Sydow. "There are no further questions."

Petrie immediately jumped to his feet. "Mr. Sparks, have you ever known the defendant to do *anything* like this before?"

Phil swung his head emphatically. "Never."

"And how long have you known her?"

"Since she's lived on the farm. Five years." He turned to face the judge. "And in all that time, Your Honor, I've never even seen Jas swat a fly. There must have been something said or done to make her so mad."

"Thank you, Mr. Sparks. That will be all for now," said Petrie.

Hat in hand, Phil slunk from the witness box. Jas let out her breath. It was over.

"We have no more witnesses, Your Honor," Mr. Sydow said. "The Commonwealth rests."

"Mr. Petrie?" The judge nodded at the public defender.

Leaning toward Jas, Petrie said in a low voice, "This is your opportunity to tell the judge your side of the story."

Jas shook her head without looking at him.

"Your Honor, the defense rests," he said in a resigned voice.

When Mr. Sydow stood to summarize his case, Jas tuned him out. She already knew Hugh had won. Phil had tried, but unless she spoke up, she would be declared guilty. Petrie had already warned her what might happen.

"Jasmine Schuler, please stand," the judge said.

Slowly, Jas and Petrie rose to their feet. The judge glanced down at the open file, then up at her. "Miss Schuler, I have no choice but to find you guilty of assault. I place you on official probation and electronic monitoring. It's also the order of the court that, since you have no relative to reside with at this time, you be placed in the custody of the Department of Social Services for placement in foster care."

The judge looked toward the back of the court. "Ms. Tomlinson, do you have a placement for this child?"

"Yes, we do, Your Honor."

"Fine. I'm reviewing this case in forty-five days. Until that time, you must abide by the special conditions stated in your rules of probation, Miss Schuler. Ms. Tomlinson, you may accompany Miss Schuler to the probation office."

The gavel banged down. Jas trained her eyes on Hugh's face, hoping he could feel her angry gaze drilling into his cheek.

Even though he'd won, she knew who was really guilty. Her grandfather hadn't put the yew branch in Whirlwind's paddock. Hugh Robicheaux had. He'd killed his own horse.

She just had to prove it.

Chapter 3

Mr. Eyler, the probation officer, read from the white sheet. "You are to report to me at least once a month. The period of time you remain on probation will depend upon your behavior."

He pointed to a line near the bottom. "Sign this statement showing that you understand the rules."

Jas forced herself to look where Mr. Eyler was pointing. Underneath the line was a space for the parent's or guardian's signature. Ms. Tomlinson, the social worker, had already signed it.

She glanced up at Ms. Tomlinson. She was a middle-aged woman with a bad perm, a red nose, and bloodshot eyes. And for the next forty-five days, this person would be responsible for her.

Picking up the pen, Jas scrawled her name.

"I'll meet with you on Friday," Mr. Eyler said,

separating the copies. He held the blue one out to Jas, who took the sheet. Ms. Tomlinson then led her out the door and into another room.

"This is Mrs. Weisgerber," Ms. Tomlinson introduced the woman sitting behind the desk. "She will be your juvenile case manager."

"I'll have *three* people checking on me?" Jas spoke aloud for the first time since she'd entered the courtroom. The sound of her voice was strange, but the idea of three people watching over her was even stranger.

Since her grandmother had died, Jas had fixed meals, cleaned the trailer, and made straight A's. Now she'd broken the law, and suddenly she needed a slew of babysitters.

"I'll be in charge of your electronic monitoring," Mrs. Weisgerber said matter-of-factly. She held up a nylon strap. Attached to it was a small black metal box. "This is your ankle bracelet and transmitter." She tapped the black box. "The transmitter 'talks' to a unit that's attached to the phone at your foster home. The unit then 'talks' to a monitoring center in Pennsylvania. The center then 'talks' to me. Every day I will receive a message that tells me if you were where you were supposed to be."

She handed the ankle bracelet to Jas, who took it cautiously, not sure what it would do.

"You must *always* wear this transmitter," Mrs. Weisgerber continued. "If you leave the specified area during lockdown times, we'll know immediately."

"Lockdown means you won't be able to leave your foster parent's house and surrounding area," Ms. Tomlinson explained as she dabbed her nose with a tissue.

Like a jail without bars, Jas thought grimly as she handed the thing back.

Mrs. Weisgerber gestured to Jas's legs. "Which ankle would you like me to put it around?"

Jas set her left foot on the seat of a chair and pulled up her pant leg. Bending, Mrs. Weisgerber slid down Jas's sock.

"It locks on directly above the anklebone." She hooked the strap around Jas's leg. "Nothing should come between the transmitter and your skin." Jas heard a snap and then felt the weight of it around her ankle, like a bell boot on a horse. "Can I get it wet?"

Mrs. Weisgerber nodded. "You can bathe, shower, even go swimming. The only thing you can't do is take it off. If you cut the bracelet or damage or lose the transmitter, you will be charged with a crime."

Slowly, Jas pulled down her pant leg and set

her foot on the floor. Her jeans covered the bracelet, but there was no way she would forget it was there.

Still talking, Mrs. Weisgerber walked back to her desk. "I will be making a schedule with you and your foster parent." She held up a piece of paper gridded with lines and labeled with the days of the week. "The schedule allows you to leave the premises at certain times."

Like I'll have someplace to go, Jas thought. High Meadows had been her home for the last five years. And now she wasn't even allowed near it. She'd never see Phil or the horses again.

A lump balled in Jas's throat. She gulped, forcing it down. There was so much at the farm that she'd miss: Phil and his sun-baked face, the new foals—Darien, Snoopy, and Jessica. And Old Sam, the dog. Would Phil remember to give him a biscuit every night before bedtime?

"I'll meet you at Miss Hahn's in half an hour," Mrs. Weisgerber said to Ms. Tomlinson.

Miss Hahn? Jas wondered. Was that her new foster parent?

"Here are directions to the house." Ms. Tomlinson ripped off a piece of paper from a small pad and handed it to Mrs. Weisgerber. "The name of her place is Second Chance Farm. It's on Springhill Road."

When they left Municipal Court, Jas half expected a deputy to escort her from the building. But she walked into the sunlight with only the tug of the bracelet to remind her she wasn't free.

Ms. Tomlinson had a beat-up county car, white with faded blue seat covers. Wadded-up tissues littered the floor. Jas slid into the passenger's seat. For a second, it felt strange not wearing handcuffs. She touched her bare wrists.

"This will be Miss Hahn's first experience as a foster parent," Ms. Tomlinson said as they drove from town. "But I think it's a perfect placement. She has horses."

Jas swung around to look at the social worker. "Horses?"

"Yes." Ms. Tomlinson smiled as if she was pleased with herself. "Quite a few. Big ones, small ones, pretty ones."

Horses! A sudden weight pressed against Jas's heart. She'd grown up with horses. She was like the wild child who'd been raised by wolves, only she'd been raised by horses. She knew their hearts, their minds, their instincts.

But ever since Whirlwind had died, something in Jas had died, too. Now she didn't know whether she could even stand being around horses again.

"What kind of horses does she have?" Jas asked several minutes later.

"I don't know. But then I don't know one horse from another," Ms. Tomlinson said as she blew her nose.

"Oh." Turning toward the window, Jas focused on the scenery. Maybe this Miss Hahn woman fox-hunted or steeplechased. Or maybe she had a breeding farm and raised Warmbloods, Arabians, or Thoroughbreds.

Jas's arms began to tingle. Okay, so maybe she was excited to be around horses again. She just hoped that Whirlwind's memory wouldn't be too painful.

"Here it is!" Ms. Tomlinson announced cheerfully.

Jas looked out the side window, almost missing the sign half-hidden by weeds. The faded black letters read S COND CHANCE ARM.

She blinked, wondering if they were at the right place. They drove up the dirt driveway, the car bouncing through ruts and exposed rock. Jas had to grab the door handle to keep from banging her head. A canopy of maple branches shaded the drive, and brambles scraped the sides of the car. Beyond the trees, Jas could see electric fence wire.

She wrinkled her nose. *Electric fence? Tacky.*

What kind of a horse farm is this?

Rolling down the window, she stuck out her head to get a better look. She couldn't tell if there were horses in the field or not because the weeds in the pasture were so tall.

"Here we are." The car jerked to a stop beside the trunk of a tree.

Leaning forward, Jas peered out the front windshield. When she saw her new home, her eyes widened in disbelief. Okay, so she hadn't expected the Robicheaux mansion, but the clapboard farmhouse in front of her was so old that the roof sagged like a swaybacked horse.

"The house could use a little TLC," Ms. Tomlinson said as she opened her car door.

"More like a bomb," Jas murmured. Barking sounds then made her glance out the side window. A pack of dogs careened around the corner of the farmhouse. A woman strode behind them, her right leg swinging stiffly.

"I hope you like dogs," Ms. Tomlinson said. Jas stared at the four mutts barking and leaping at her car door. "Uh, I actually do." Besides Old Sam, Hugh had purebred Jack Russell Terriers.

"Reese, sit. Tilly, sit," the woman commanded as she came up to the car. "Angel, sit. Lassie, sit."

The four mutts consisted of a big tan one, a fat black one, a longhaired pointy-nosed one, and some kind of hound. They all sat immediately.

Jas's gaze shifted from the dogs to the woman standing behind them, her thumbs hooked in the deep pockets of her overalls. She was as tall and broad-shouldered as a man. Her black hair was laced with gray and pulled back into a ponytail.

"Hello, Miss Hahn," Ms. Tomlinson greeted as she walked around the front of the car. "I'd like you to meet Jasmine Schuler."

"Jas," Jas said through the open window.

"Hello, Jas." Miss Hahn smiled. Her eyes were nut-brown, her skin tan, her face a road map of wrinkles. Straddling the dogs, she pulled open the car door.

Jas swung her legs out. The dogs quivered in excitement but didn't break their sit command. Jas held out her hand for them to sniff, and they then burst into a wiggling mass of tails and tongues.

"Once they get a good whiff, they'll leave you alone." Miss Hahn peered into the backseat of the car. "Got any things to bring in?"

"Just a bag of clothes."

"Jas isn't allowed back on the farm where she was living before," Ms. Tomlinson explained. Grabbing a tissue from her purse, she sneezed. "Allergies," she apologized. "Before I leave, I'll get a list of things that need to be picked up at her grandfather's trailer. Anything else will have to be bought from her clothes allowance."

"Clothes allowance. Right." Miss Hahn nodded. "I'm new at this foster-parent stuff, Jas, so you'll have to bear with me."

I'm new at it, too, Jas thought, *and already I don't like it.* Her gaze dropped to the dogs. The black sausage-shaped one licked her fingers while the yellowish retriever thrust a soggy tennis ball at her.

The retriever's gray-sprinkled muzzle looked just like Old Sam's. Jas began to wonder if her longtime buddy was waiting for her and her grandfather to come home. If he was, he was in for a letdown.

Jas closed her eyes and forced back the sadness. What if she never saw Old Sam again?

Suddenly, she pictured her grandfather lying on the ground, the medical technicians hovering over him. What if her grandfather died and she wasn't there to say good-bye?

No, that won't happen. It can't. Jas blinked back tears. *Grandfather will be all right, he'll get out of the nursing home, and we'll be together again.*

Until then, Jas would make sure that Miss Hahn, Ms. Tomlinson, and Mr. Eyler understood that she had to see him. And soon. Not only did she love him unconditionally, but he was all she had left.

Chapter 4

"Woof!" A bark jerked Jas from her thoughts. The retriever plopped the slimy ball in her lap.

Picking it up carefully, Jas tossed the ball into a tangle of forsythia bushes. When the retriever hopped after it, she noticed he had only three legs.

"Watch out or Reese will want you to do that all day," Miss Hahn said. She was studying Jas curiously.

Jas glanced away. She might be forced to live with the woman, but that didn't mean she had to like her.

"We can discuss Jas's placement over lunch," Ms. Tomlinson said. "Make sure everybody understands the rules."

Leaning over the backseat, Jas retrieved the grocery bag. Miss Hahn led them around to the back of the farmhouse. As they walked down the cracked sidewalk, Jas craned her neck, trying to see the barn or a horse, but a weather-beaten shed and overgrown bushes were blocking the way.

Miss Hahn opened the screen door and ushered them into the kitchen. Jas tripped over an empty dog bowl. A huge oak table filled the small room, making it hard to find a place to stand.

"Sit anywhere you like," Miss Hahn instructed, waving at the six mismatched chairs. She walked over to the refrigerator and pulled out two platters. One platter was heaped with cold cuts. The other had slices of tomato and apple, bunches of grapes, and plump strawberries.

"Um, I'm not hungry," Jas said quickly.

"Are you sure?" Ms. Tomlinson raised her eyebrows. "Doesn't everything look delicious?"

"I'd rather go to my room." Jas crunched the bag to her chest.

I want to be alone.

"Okay. You'll like your room, Jas," Ms. Tomlinson said. "It overlooks a pond."

"We have to share a bath, and there's no air conditioning," Miss Hahn hastily added. "But the trees make enough shade so that it's not too hot."

Jas didn't respond. It was as if Ms. Tomlinson and Miss Hahn were trying to convince themselves that this was a swell setup. But Jas didn't care. She was here only to do her forty-five days.

She didn't have to like it if she didn't want to.

"I'll show you to your room," said Miss Hahn. Jas followed her through the living room and up a flight of wooden steps to an upstairs bedroom.

The room was furnished with a single bed, a dresser, a bedside table, and a reading light. When Jas walked across the bare wooden floor, her footsteps echoed.

Pretty lonely-looking room, Jas thought.

Miss Hahn brushed off the bottom of the worn quilt that covered the bed. "Cat hairs. If you don't want the cats in here, you'll have to keep the door shut. Fluffy and Tuff think this is their room. The bathroom's down the hall." She pointed her thumb to the right. "Towels are in the cupboard. This place was built before closets were invented, so you'll have to keep everything in the dresser."

"Thank you," Jas said, forcing herself to be polite.

The doorbell rang. "That must be Mrs. Weisgerber." Miss Hahn turned to go, then hesitated in the doorway.

"I'll be down in a minute," Jas said, wanting her to leave. "I want to unpack my, uh, bag," she stammered, realizing that she barely had anything in it.

"Okay," Miss Hahn said as she nervously smoothed a strand of hair behind her ear. It then occurred to Jas that the older woman was feeling as awkward as she was.

"I'd prefer it if you called me Diane," Miss Hahn continued.

"And I'd prefer not to," Jas said, just softly enough so that Miss Hahn couldn't hear. Calling her by a first name might imply they were going to be friends.

When Miss Hahn left, Jas looked around the tiny room. The trailer she and her grandfather had lived in hadn't been huge, but it was comfortable and homey. Jas's own room had been perfect. Ribbons and trophies covered one wall, and shelves of stuffed animals crisscrossed the other. The animals spilled over the desk that Jas always tried to keep clear for schoolwork.

This room looks nothing like mine. It's going to need a dozen cats to fill it up, thought Jas.

She set the paper bag on the dresser, then took out her clothes. Whirlwind's photo fluttered to the floor. Picking it up, she slid it in the back pocket of her jeans. She didn't want anyone to see it. She didn't want to have to explain what had happened to the beautiful mare.

Pulling open the bottom dresser drawer, Jas neatly stacked her jeans, underpants, and T-shirt on one side. Even with all her clothes unpacked, the drawer still looked empty.

"Jas?" Ms. Tomlinson called up the stairs. Her voice was so loud it sounded as if the woman was right behind her. The house was pretty small, and it reminded Jas of the crowded detention center.

Jas realized how good she had had it at High Meadows. Phil and Grandfather had been so busy that she'd been left alone much of the time. And although Hugh instructed her when she rode his horses, there were long chunks of time when she could escape into a pasture to play with the foals or into the loft to read and daydream. She had so much freedom and time to herself.

"Jas!" Ms. Tomlinson's voice howled down the hall.

Jas made a disgusted face. Obviously, those carefree days were over. With her ankle bracelet and four babysitters, private moments would be impossible.

"I'll be down in a minute!" she hollered. "I have to use the bathroom."

She closed the drawer and folded up the bag. Then she walked down the hall toward the bathroom, treading softly so her tennis shoes didn't clump on the wood planks.

When she passed an open doorway, she stopped and peeked inside. A double bed was neatly made with a wedding ring–patterned quilt and piles of squishy pillows. Framed antique lace hung on the walls, and potted plants dangled from macramé holders in front of the long windows. Several framed photos of horses were on the dresser.

Leaning backward into the hall, she listened for the sound of voices downstairs. The three ladies seemed to be chatting amiably.

On tiptoes, Jas hurried to the dresser and picked up the largest photo. It was a professional shot of a horse and rider going over a jump at a horse show. Jas had had dozens of them taken of her and Whirlwind.

Jas studied the photo, trying to decide if the rider was Miss Hahn. The horse was definitely a Thoroughbred, a sleek bay with its knees high and square. Jas could tell it wasn't taken recently, since the cut of the hunt coat was too long, and when she glanced at the corner date tag, it read WASHINGTON INTERNATIONAL HORSE SHOW 1983.

The International. Still one of the toughest shows around.

She picked up a second picture of three horses cantering across a field. Yearlings, Jas decided, long-legged, wild-eyed, and bursting with vitality.

Suddenly, Jas heard a familiar sound.

A horse's whinny from outside made her

glance up. Pushing aside the fern fronds, she looked out the window, her heart catching in her throat at the sound of an answering whinny.

Horses! But the thick maple boughs from the trees surrounding the house made it impossible to see. Still, she knew they were out there.

"Jas!" someone called from the bottom of the stairs. She quickly put down the photo. She was turning to leave when a third picture, half hidden by a wooden box, caught her attention.

It was of the same bay horse, with a woman holding it. Looking closer, Jas realized that it was Miss Hahn, only twenty years younger. But what made her almost fall to the ground was the man who was standing to the side with a sport cap angled on his head and a hunt whip in his hand.

It was a younger version of Hugh Robicheaux.

Jas heard footsteps coming up the stairs. "Jas!" This time the voice was more insistent. By the time Ms. Tomlinson reached the top of the steps, Jas was walking steadily down the hall, even though her legs were trembling.

Miss Hahn knew Hugh?

"Please don't keep us waiting. Mrs. Weisgerber and I have other appointments," Ms. Tomlinson explained as she herded Jas down the steps.

In the living room, Mrs. Weisgerber was hooking up the black flat rectangular computer unit to the phone. Jas glanced warily at Miss Hahn, who was sitting on the sofa eating a sandwich.

Did Miss Hahn really know Hugh?

"The transmitter on Jas's ankle 'talks' to this unit, much like a cordless telephone communicates with its base," Mrs. Weisgerber was telling Miss Hahn. Ms. Tomlinson was seated on a ladder-back chair, a plate of food balanced on her lap.

Slowly, Jas perched on the seat of a rocking chair. *Get a grip,* she told herself sternly.

Of course Miss Hahn knew Hugh. They were both horse people. Both about the same age. They'd probably competed against each other at one time. But that was a long time ago, Jas reasoned.

"The unit reports to a monitoring center in Harrisburg, Pennsylvania, through the phone line," Mrs. Weisgerber continued. "The Harrisburg center faxes their reports to me *unless* they receive a signal of tampering or violation. Then they'll call me directly. Tampering means that someone has messed with the ankle bracelet. Violation means that Jas is not where she is supposed to be."

The photo was old, Jas continued. *But still, should I tell Ms. Tomlinson that this Miss Hahn person knows the man I "assaulted"?*

The picture didn't really prove anything. Hugh could have been just a bystander at the show. Besides, ever since Jas's mother had left when she was a baby and her grandmother had died a year ago, Jas had taken care of herself. So she figured that she didn't need Ms. Tomlinson's help now.

Ms. Tomlinson picked up a sheet of paper on the coffee table. "We have made up a tentative schedule," she said, handing the paper to Jas. She stared at it. Under each day of the week was listed the date and the hours of the day.

Mrs. Weisgerber stuck a key into the back of the unit and turned. "There, your bracelet is on. I'll fax the schedule to Harrisburg," she explained. "From now on, this unit"–she placed her hand on the box–"will keep track of where you are, Jas. That means you need to be where you're supposed to be, especially during lock-down times."

Jas reluctantly read the horrible schedule. MAY was written in big letters between 7:30 and 9:00 A.M., and again from 4:00 to 6:00 P.M. That meant Jas could move about freely. The rest of the time was mostly LOCK, which meant she had to be close to the monitor.

"Every Monday, we'll meet to complete the new week's schedule," Mrs. Weisgerber continued.

"Can visits to my grandfather be built into the schedule?" Jas asked.

"Your grandfather's very ill, Jas," Ms. Tomlinson said gently.

"That's all the more reason to see him."

"Fine, we'll try to fit it into the schedule," Ms. Tomlinson said. "Of course, your visits will depend on how well you follow the rules of probation."

Jas swung to look at her. "What do you mean?"

"In a foster care situation, everyone has to do his or her part to make things work."

Jas looked first at Miss Hahn, then at Mrs. Weisgerber, then back at Ms. Tomlinson. Just like Hugh Robicheaux, the three women were forcing her to make a deal.

A sour taste filled Jas's mouth. She knew she had no choice. If she didn't follow the rules, she might never see Grandfather again.

Jas pushed herself back in the rocking chair. "I understand," she said flatly.

A movement under the sofa caught her attention. A tabby cat glared at her with yellow eyes. Jas glared back. The cat lay flat against the floor, as if afraid to come out.

Little kitty's trapped, Jas thought as she began to pump the rocker furiously.

Just like me.

Then the cat slunk from under the sofa and, tail between its legs, skittered from the room to freedom.

Chapter 5

"We'll have to figure out something for you to do during lockdown times," Miss Hahn said to Jas.

Jas gripped the arms of the chair and pushed down hard.

"She enjoys reading," Ms. Tomlinson said. "We can schedule trips to the library."

"Good." Miss Hahn sounded relieved. "We can hit the public library first thing tomorrow–" Suddenly, her tan cheeks colored slightly. "I mean," she started again, then hesitated and finally glanced at Ms. Tomlinson for help.

The social worker took the schedule and began erasing. "We can do a trip to the library. Once a week, Tuesday after lunch, how's that sound?"

"Oh, just dandy," Jas muttered under her breath.

"We've arranged to have your MAY times coincide with Miss Hahn's feeding schedule," Ms. Tomlinson continued.

"I'm hoping you'll help around the farm," Miss Hahn explained.

Jas kept her eyes on her lap. MUST, MAY, LOCK-DOWN. For the next week, her life would be boringly mapped out for her. It was like a huge, sick prank that some vengeful person was playing on her.

If she had been back at High Meadows, her summer would be filled with horses. She'd be busy from dawn to dusk riding, gentling foals, and grooming. Every weekend, she'd be going to a big show. Whirlwind had been on her way to winning the Junior Horse of the Year Award for their zone, and she'd been racking up points in equitation classes.

But Whirlwind was dead and none of that mattered anymore.

"I think that's all we have to discuss," Mrs. Weisgerber said, gathering her things to leave.

Ms. Tomlinson wiped her mouth with a napkin. "Mr. Eyler will be here Friday morning. And don't hesitate to call me if there are any problems," she said to Miss Hahn. "And thank you for a delicious lunch."

"You're welcome." Miss Hahn stood up. "Jas, would you like a tour of the farm?"

"Is it in my schedule?" she asked sarcastically. Ms. Tomlinson checked her watch. "That's right. She can't leave the house until four."

"Oh, right." Hastily, Miss Hahn picked up the two plates. "Chase will be here then."

Chase? Was that a person's name?

"He's helping me out this summer. He's about your age, Jas. I'm sure he'd be happy to give you a tour."

"What I'd really like is a shower," Jas said, plucking at a greasy strand of hair.

"Good idea," Ms. Tomlinson said, and after repeating several more do's and don'ts, she and Mrs. Weisgerber left.

Jas stood up. "The shower?" She repeated to Miss Hahn.

"Right. You'll find everything you'll need in the bathroom."

"Okay." Jas hurried upstairs and into her room, startling a calico cat curled on the foot of the bed. For a second, the two eyed each other. Then the calico rolled over and stretched.

Jas ruffled the soft tummy. "You must be the friendly one." The calico purred, and the room didn't seem quite so lonely.

Jas took out clean jeans, a T-shirt, and underwear. *Ms. Tomlinson better remember my riding clothes when she goes to the trailer,* Jas thought. Not that she expected to ever wear them again, but just being able to hold and smell them would be nice.

Jas walked into the bathroom, immediately locking the door and slumping against it with relief. She'd hated the group showers at the center. That's why her hair was so dirty.

But a sudden ache in her bladder made her realize how badly she had to pee. As she unzipped her jeans and made her way to the toilet, a noise startled her. It instantly reminded her of the center, where even going to the bathroom was risky.

At the center, she had had to sit on the toilet with her feet drawn up. That way, the tough gangs of girls who prowled the halls and bathrooms hunting for someone to hassle wouldn't see her.

Jas listened. When she realized the sound was a vehicle coming up the drive, her heart slowed in relief.

When she finished going to the bathroom, Jas pulled off her T-shirt and underwear. Automatically, her hands covered her breasts, shielding them. A warm breeze came through the slatted shutters of the bathroom window and she shivered.

It was the first time she'd been naked in two weeks. At the center, she'd slept in the same shirt she wore all day. That way, she never had to completely undress in front of anyone.

She turned on the shower. As she waited for the water to get hot, Jas studied herself in the mirror. Since glass mirrors were forbidden at the center, she hadn't seen herself in a long time.

Now she didn't recognize the pale-faced, sad-eyed girl who stared back at her. Had she changed that much in only three weeks?

When the mirror steamed up, Jas stepped into the tub. The hot water pelted her skin and hair, washing away weeks of dirt. Jas let her eyelids drift shut.

For a moment, she forgot about everything–Whirlwind, the trial, her grandfather, Hugh. But then a blast of cold water made her eyes pop open.

She *couldn't* forget. Not if she was going to prove that Hugh had killed Whirlwind.

Scrubbing hard, Jas washed every inch of her skin, the nylon bracelet around her ankle growing dark with water. When she was finished with her body, she started on her hair. Jas noticed that Miss Hahn had luxurious scented shampoo in the shower, so she poured some on her palm, breathing in the fragrance before lathering her hair.

After rinsing, she turned off the shower and wrapped a soft towel around her. As she stepped from the tub, a knock on the door made her jump.

"Jas? You have a phone call. A Dr. Aladdin. He needs to talk to you about your grandfather."

Jas's heart quickened. "Is Grandfather all right?"

"Yes. Dr. Aladdin says he's recovering nicely. You can use the phone in the living room—the one the monitor's hooked up to."

"Thanks. Tell him I'll be there in one minute." Excited, Jas dried herself and dressed. Twisting the towel around her head like a turban, she thumped barefoot down the steps. As she picked up the receiver, she heard the clinking of dishes in the kitchen.

"Hello? Dr. Aladdin?"

"Jas."

Jas's mouth went dry. From just that one word, the honey-smooth voice speaking her name, she knew who was on the other end.

Hugh Robicheaux.

Jas turned her back to the kitchen door. "How did you know I was here?"

He chuckled softly. "I'll *always* know where you are and what you're doing."

Goose bumps prickled Jas's damp skin. She covered the mouthpiece, hoping he wouldn't hear her sharp intake of breath.

How did he know?

"Aren't you going to ask me what I want?"

Hugh asked, his tone as nasty as a spoiled brat.

"What do you want?" Jas repeated, trying to keep her voice from trembling.

"I want you to remember our deal."

"I do. But only if you keep your part of it. Grandfather better be getting the best care possible."

"He is."

"Where is he?"

"That's for the dauntless Ms. Tomlinson to tell you." Hugh chuckled. "Good-bye, Jas. Oh, and say hello to Diane for me."

Jas froze. "You know Miss Hahn?" she hissed. "Is that how you found out I was living here?" But he had already hung up.

Slowly, Jas replaced the receiver. Turning her head slightly, she listened to the familiar sounds coming from the kitchen. The slam of the cupboard door and the whoosh of running water sent chills up her spine.

The photo hadn't lied. Hugh did know Miss Hahn. That's how he knew where she was living. And that's why he'd always know what she was doing.

Miss Hahn was reporting everything to him.

Chapter 6

Doubling over, Jas dropped into the rocker. She covered her mouth, stifling a moan. She had to tell someone that Hugh knew Miss Hahn.

Could she trust Ms. Tomlinson?

No way. The social worker would think Jas was making it up. Besides, Hugh had mentioned Ms. Tomlinson's name. Maybe they were *all* in it together. Stanford was a small town, and Hugh's family had been its original founders. Not only did he have connections, he knew everybody.

Oh, Grandfather, Jas whispered. *What should I do?*

A sudden thought struck Jas. If Hugh needed to spy on her, it meant that he had *definitely* killed Whirlwind. But why would he want to kill his own horse?

Whirlwind had been in her showing prime, worth over a hundred thousand dollars. Even if she'd injured herself, Hugh could have bred her and made lots of money off the foals. It just didn't make sense that he would want her dead.

Until she had proof, Jas knew she couldn't tell anyone her suspicions. Maybe being at Second Chance Farm was actually to her advantage. Maybe Miss Hahn would somehow lead her to the answer to why Hugh had killed Whirlwind.

Footsteps. Without moving, Jas directed her gaze toward the kitchen. Miss Hahn stood in the doorway, her large frame filling it.

"How's your grandfather?" she asked, her voice so sincere Jas almost doubted her ears. If she and Hugh were in cahoots, she *had* to have known it wasn't a doctor on the phone.

"He's doing better," Jas replied, surprised at her composure. "Dr. Aladdin–"

Jas caught her breath. Dr. *Aladdin.* Aladdin was the name of a horse that died the year Jas and her grandparents came to High Meadows Farm. She was only eight years old, and the sight of the dead horse lying in the stall sent her crying into her grandfather's arms.

Why would Hugh use that name?

With an effort, Jas refocused her attention on Miss Hahn. "The doctor said that from now on, he would be communicating through Ms. Tomlinson," Jas explained calmly. "He was just checking to see if I had any other relatives."

Miss Hahn leaned against the door frame, her head cocked. "Oh."

Jas could see the question in her eyes. But there was no way she was saying anything else. She would *never* give Miss Hahn anything to report to Hugh.

Abruptly, she stood up. "May I borrow a hair dryer? Until Ms. Tomlinson brings my things, I'm going to have to use yours. If that's okay."

"Help yourself. Everything's under the bathroom sink."

"Thanks," Jas said as she dashed up the stairs.

"Chase is here," Miss Hahn called after her. "He said he'd be happy to show you around. It's about three forty-five now, so you have some time."

"Okay," Jas called back, controlling the quiver in her voice. Sprinting into the bathroom, she slammed and locked the door.

Sitting on the toilet seat, Jas cradled her face in her hands, squeezing her fingers against her temples.

Aladdin. Whirlwind. This doesn't make sense.

But one thing Jas knew for sure: no matter how nice Miss Hahn acted, she couldn't trust her. She couldn't trust *anybody*.

Loud whistling suddenly made her freeze.

Someone was in the backyard, walking up the sidewalk to the porch.

"Hey, Tilly, hey, Angel. Where's Lassie? Good boy, Reese."

It was a guy's voice. Lifting a slat in the shutter, Jas peered out the window, catching a glimpse of the top of a baseball cap. Then the cap disappeared from view, and she heard the slam of the screen door.

Chase, I guess.

Bending down, Jas took the dryer and brush from under the sink. When her hair was dry, she stared in surprise at her image in the mirror.

Her brown hair had grown. She'd always worn it short so she could cram it under a riding helmet. Now it fell softly against her cheeks, framing her face like a shimmery curtain.

"Jas! Chase is here!"

Quickly, she put the dryer back, hung up the towel, brushed her teeth with toothpaste and a finger, and combed her hair one last time. She knew she had to act normal. She couldn't let on to Miss Hahn that she knew what was up.

Hurrying into her room, she put on clean socks and sneakers. As she walked down the hall, she glanced at her ankle. The transmitter was bulging out.

Miss Hahn was still in the kitchen putting

food away. A guy about Jas's age was leaning against the counter, his legs crossed at the ankles, talking with Miss Hahn as if they were old buddies.

"Blue's broken his halter again," he was telling her, and when he launched into the tale of trying to catch the horse, Jas had a chance to study him.

He was tall and lanky, wearing a tank top tucked into faded jeans slung low on his hips. His arms were tan and sinewy with muscles, as if he worked outside a lot. But what Jas really noticed was the laughter in his voice when he talked about Blue. She could tell that he loved horses, too.

"Here's Jas," Miss Hahn said.

The guy straightened and turned to look at her. The bill of his baseball cap shaded his face, but Jas could still feel his gaze.

She flushed, suddenly feeling awkward, as if he were a date. Not that she'd ever had one before. He was probably staring at her because she was the freaky foster kid.

"Hi," he finally said.

Nervous, Jas shoved her fingers in her jean pockets. "Hi."

"I'd go with you on the grand tour, but I have to make a few phone calls," Miss Hahn said.

"Chase can explain the chores. I'm not sure who's on the schedule to help feed." She directed her statement to Chase, who was ready to head out. "I hope Jas will want to help," she added. "She has lots of experience with horses,"

"I think Lucy's working," Chase said as he strode across the kitchen. He pushed open the screen door, holding it for a second, then letting it go, as if he didn't want to appear too polite.

Jas noticed the gesture, then hurried after him, the dogs following behind. Chase was about a foot taller than she was, and his stride was long. Jas lengthened her own stride, cursing when she tripped over Angel, who zigzagged in front of her.

When they reached the edge of the yard, Chase didn't even glance over his shoulder as he silently headed up the drive.

So much for friendly conversation, Jas thought, glowering at his back. Not that she cared. She was glad to get away from Miss Hahn's spying eyes. And she'd rather see the horses than talk to some kid.

Still, she couldn't help wonder if Chase rode. If Miss Hahn bred and raised horses, he might help start them under saddle, something she'd just started doing before...

She pushed the thought out of her mind, concentrating instead on her growing excitement as they approached a heavy metal gate set in stained three-board fencing. Chase wound through a pass-through built in the fence. It was designed to let humans in and keep horses from getting out.

Jas followed, her underarms sweating from the heat and anticipation. When she got to the other side of the fence, she stopped in her tracks.

Before her stood barns, sheds, patched-up fences, makeshift paddocks, and wandering animals. There were burros, goats, geese, cows, chickens, llamas, peacocks, and pigs.

Her mouth fell open in disbelief. This wasn't a horse farm. It was Noah's Ark.

As soon as the burros saw Chase, they ambled over, their long ears flopping. Ignoring the animals, Angel and Reese bounded off into an overgrown field. Lassie trotted toward the geese. A goat appeared and thrust his muzzle into Jas's palm.

"Little devil's looking for treats," Chase said as he patted the burros, then continued toward a small metal building. Jas hurried after him, trying to keep from stepping on the geese who waddled around her legs while Lassie barked behind them.

Suddenly the goat grabbed the hem of her T-shirt with his teeth. "Hey!" Jas pushed him away. Lowering his head, he butted her in the thigh.

Chase grinned. "He won't hurt you," he said as he went up two concrete steps and opened the door of the ramshackle building. "He just gets frisky sometimes."

Only the goat's friskiness *did* hurt. Jas rubbed her thigh, then leaped up the steps after him.

"This is the office." He waved his arm around the small room.

"The off—whoa!" Suddenly, the two burros climbed up the steps, forcing Jas backward. She collided with Chase, stepping on his toes.

"Whoops, sorry!" Embarrassed, she jumped sideways and knocked over a desk chair.

"That's all right. Heckle, Jeckle, get out of here," Chase scolded the two burros. Shooing them off the steps, he shut the door halfway.

Jas grabbed the chair at the same time that Chase reached for it, and they bumped heads. "Oh, gosh, sorry again!" Jas jerked upright, horrified. How could she be such a klutz?

Chase grinned. "No damage done. See?" He rapped on the top of his cap-covered head. "Actually, *I* should apologize. Heckle and Jeckle usually have better manners, but it's dinnertime and they get rowdy when they're hungry. Plus, this weekend we had a bunch of kids from a day camp, and they spoiled them rotten with treats."

"Day camp? I don't understand." Confused, Jas looked around. The small office had two desks overflowing with papers, manila folders, half-empty soda cans, and books. Three file cabinets lined one wall, folding chairs were on the other, and photos and posters of animals were tacked everywhere.

Jas tried to compare this dusty, disorganized room with Phil's immaculate office in the barn at High Meadows. So far, Second Chance Farm was nothing like any horse farm she'd ever seen.

She looked questioningly at Chase, who was slouched against one of the file cabinets. He held a clipboard in one hand, but his eyes were watching her.

"Isn't this a horse farm?" she asked.

"We do have horses. Twenty of them."

"But what about all the other animals?"

Chase snorted. "You mean you thought this was a *horse* horse farm like the fancy Thoroughbred places on Mill Road?"

High Meadows Farm was on Mill Road.

"Well...yes."

"Ha, that's pretty funny." Chase smacked the clipboard against his thigh.

Jas didn't think it was funny at all. "So then,

what kind of a *horse* farm is it?" she asked mockingly.

"Well, it's not *that* kind of a *horse* farm," he replied, his tone just as mocking. "It's a farm for rescued animals. You know, like the Humane Society. The animal shelter." Chase leaned forward, gesturing with one hand as if he were talking to one of the little kids from the day camp. "We take in animals that no one else wants."

"Oh." Jas nodded once, her blood beginning to boil because of his tone. "Rejects. Now I get it."

And did she ever. No wonder he'd been studying her so intently.

Cheeks reddening, Jas stepped toward him. "Now I know why you're staring at me like I'm a sideshow freak," she said, her fists clenched by her side. "You're thinking how I fit in perfectly with the animals at Second Chance Farm. The only difference is, I'm a *person* no one else wants!"

Chapter 7

Jas glared up at Chase, her body bristling like a mad cat's.

"Wrong," Chase said as he dropped the clipboard on top of the file cabinet and glared right back. "We don't think of the animals as rejects. They're here because people are stupid and greedy and cruel. I was staring at you because–" Suddenly, he flushed bright red. "Never mind."

Turning abruptly, he picked up the clipboard, flipped back a page and busily scanned it.

Jas felt her cheeks grow hot. Was he about to say "because you're cute"?

Jas stopped to think for a second. She knew it wasn't his fault she was here. She shouldn't have gotten so mad at him. "Oh, well, I'm sorry I got so mad," she said.

Chase looked over at her. Jas dropped her gaze to the floor, feeling totally stupid.

Suddenly, Angel, Lassie, and Reese shoved the door open and charged into the office. Their tails thumped against the desks. As Jas bent to pat them, she blew out a shaky breath.

"Hee-haw!" An ear-splitting bray made her twist around. The two burros, Heckle and Jeckle, stood in the doorway, front hooves propped on the office floor, hind legs on the bottom step.

"All right, we're coming." Chase checked the clock on the wall. "Lucy should be here any second to help feed. It takes a while with all the different animals."

"I'll help," Jas said, immediately wondering why she was volunteering to work. She didn't owe Miss Hahn and her farm anything.

"Good, we need all the help we can get," he said. Pushing past Heckle and Jeckle, Chase bounded down the steps.

Jas followed, but immediately slipped in something gray and squishy. Lifting her foot, she checked the sole of her sneaker.

Great. Goose poop.

"We'll start with the horses," Chase called, striding ahead.

Jas hurried after him. Okay, so she'd acted like a dork. But she was thirteen and had zero experience with guys. It wasn't so unusual.

But what about Chase? Was he really about to say she was cute?

No way. Not me.

Jas shook her head. He was probably going to say he was staring because he'd never seen a foster kid before.

She bit her lip hard. What a fool she was. She'd been around the center punks for so long that she'd forgotten what a "normal" kid might think about someone like her.

Breaking into a jog, Jas tried to catch up with Chase, who'd disappeared inside a barn. She needed to forget about him and think about the horses.

Horses. She grinned excitedly. Okay, so they weren't going to be sleek Thoroughbreds or majestic Trakehners. But they'd have four legs and whinny, and maybe–just maybe–there'd be one to ride. Not that any horse would ever come close to Whirlwind.

When she reached the barn, Jas slowed and stared at it in dismay. The rectangular building looked like an abandoned warehouse. The paint was peeling, and the aisle door hung on one hinge. Hesitantly, she stepped inside.

"Down here!" Chase hollered from somewhere at the other end. "I'm in the feed room."

"In a minute!" Jas wasn't about to rush past the stalls, which were arranged on both sides of the dirt aisle. In the summer at High Meadows, they'd brought the horses inside during the day.

They'd covered them with fly sheets and fed them the best alfalfa hay there was. Sprayers automatically spritzed repellent from the ceiling, and fans stirred the air. It was a four-star hotel for horses.

From what Jas could see, the accommodations at Second Chance Farm had no stars. Still, the barn was cool and dark against the heat and bugs of summer.

The first stall Jas glanced into was empty. It was clean, however, and bedded with thick straw. In the second stall, a horse dozed behind a mesh door, his brown eyes half closed.

"Hey." Jas reached one finger through the mesh, eager to feel the velvety soft muzzle. Startled, the horse jerked his head up, and Jas got a better look at him.

He was so thin, she could count every rib, and when she looked at his back, she gasped.

A bone was sticking out.

Jas gagged. Grabbing hold of her stomach, she stumbled backward, slamming into the wall behind her.

"The Animal Control Officer found him locked in a stall," Chase said as he walked up the aisle, a bucket in each hand. "The manure was piled so high around his legs he couldn't move."

Jas clapped a hand over her mouth. Turning,

she rushed from the barn and threw up her breakfast in a patch of weeds outside the door.

Chase was quiet, and she didn't hear him come up beside her. "Here." He handed her a can of soda. "This might help."

She took a quick sip, letting the syrupy drink wash away the terrible taste in her mouth. "Why didn't you warn me?" she yelled.

He shrugged. "I'm sorry. I wasn't thinking. Usually we prepare visitors by telling them ahead of time the story behind each horse. This horse here, Ruffles, just came off quarantine yesterday, so I didn't know that Diane, I mean Miss Hahn, moved him into this barn."

Jas pressed the cold soda can to her forehead. Her skin felt clammy. "Has the vet seen him?"

"The animal control officer called the vet immediately. Before he came here, Ruffles was in a barn full of fat, well-cared-for Morgan horses. But about a month ago, he threw his owner's daughter. Locking him in his stall with no food for four weeks was his punishment."

"No—no way." Jas swung her head. "People don't do things like that."

But you know they do, a voice inside her head said. *Hugh killed Whirlwind, remember?*

Jas began to feel sick again. Stumbling to the shady side of the barn, she propped herself against the wall and closed her eyes.

"Hey, Chase, what's going on?" a cheerful voice asked.

Snapping her eyes open, Jas saw a girl waltzing toward them. Reese and Lassie trotted beside her with adoring expressions on their doggy faces. And no wonder. Tall and shapely as a cover girl, with shoulder-length blond hair, she was a very attractive girl.

"Hey, Luce." Chase shoved his hands in his jean pockets, his expression as sheepishly adoring as the dogs'. "This is Jas, Miss Hahn's, uh—" He stopped, as if not sure what to say.

"Foster kid," Jas helped him out, looking at Lucy with a very unadoring expression. Lucy was about fifteen or sixteen, Jas figured, just the right age for wrapping a younger guy like Chase around her finger.

"Hi, Jas." Lucy eyed her up and down, then jerked her head toward the weeds. "I see you just blew lunch. Must be Miss Hahn's cooking."

"She just met Ruffles," Chase said.

"Couldn't take it, huh?" Hands in her back pockets, Lucy rocked on the heels of her paddock boots and thrust out her amply rounded breasts. "All the greenhorns have trouble. You'll get used to it."

Greenhorn! Jas balled her fingers into a fist,

wishing she could punch Lucy in her adorable little face. But she smiled instead. "Yup, that's me. Never seen a horse close up."

Chase gave her a puzzled look.

"So, Chase, I thought you were going to show me how to feed," Jas said. "What do the horses eat? Straw?"

"Straw!" Lucy tilted her head and laughed, showing off even, white teeth. "Good luck training *her*, Chase," she said as she headed back to the office, calling, "If you're feeding the horses, I'll do the rest."

When Lucy left, Jas blew out her breath and strode back into the barn, halting in front of Ruffles's stall. This time she studied every skinny, moth-eaten inch of him.

"He's a lot better than when he first came," Chase said. "The bone is sticking up because the vet had to cut away—"

Jas clapped her hands to her ears. "I don't want to hear about it just yet," she said. "And how can you be so calm about something like this?"

"I want to be a vet."

"Oh, I should have guessed." Dropping her hands from her ears, Jas walked down the aisle, glancing into the rest of the stalls. Hollow-eyed horses with rough coats, knock-knees, and ewe-necks stared back at her.

Jas pressed her lips together, trying not to feel revulsion. The stalls at High Meadows had held such perfect horses, their coats groomed to a satiny patina. Their manes were pulled to just the right length, their tails brushed full and smooth, and each wore color-coordinated fly sheets and leg protectors.

But this bunch...Jas couldn't find the right words to describe them.

Chase had been following silently behind her. When she stopped abruptly, he was so close, he almost fell over her.

"I don't get it," she said. "They're in such terrible shape, why doesn't the vet just put them down?"

Chase frowned. "What do you mean?"

"Well, what good are they?" Jas waved her hand at the row of stalls. "Their medical care must cost a fortune, and I bet it takes forever to get them healthy again. Then you still have a horse that will never show or race or even be good enough to breed."

Chase's frown turned sharper. "Oh, now I get it. You're a horse snob."

"A horse snob?" Jas repeated in disbelief.

"Yeah. One of those la-de-da types who love the ribbons and trophies and admiring glances when their horse wins something. The kind whose egos depend on reading their names in the *Chronicle of the Horse*. They don't really love horses, they only love how much they're worth."

Jas narrowed her eyes. How dare the jerk accuse her of not loving horses!

"You are so wrong," she shot back. "Not that I *care* what you think. I'm here at this stupid farm because I have to be. I'll do my time and then I'm out of here. So don't try and give me any grief!" Whirling, Jas plunged from the barn, charging through the geese, scattering them as she strode past the office. The door was open, and Tilly sat on the top step, panting. Jas bet that Miss Hahn was inside, talking on the phone.

Breaking into a jog, she swung around the pass-through and into the shady backyard. She plopped under a big maple and buried her face in her arms. When she was certain she was alone, she burst into tears. Not only had the day been one of the worst in her life, but now she was stuck at this Noah's Ark for rejects.

A wet nose pushed its way under her arm. "Go away," Jas sobbed. But when the wet nose nudged more insistently, she peered over her arms. Lassie was staring at her, wagging her tail happily. Flopping on the ground, she rolled over against Jas's leg and thumped her tail harder.

"Fine. I'll scratch you." Jas wiped her damp

cheeks on her shirt sleeve. Then, sniffing noisily, she rubbed the dog's fat tummy until Lassie's hind foot flailed the air.

A sudden movement by the fence caught her eye. Miss Hahn was peering over the gate. When she saw Jas looking back, she turned and walked away.

She's spying, Jas thought. Anger began to dry her tears. According to the schedule, Jas wasn't on lockdown right now.

She could run free or even walk away. She could run to Springhill Road and hitch a ride to High Meadows Farm to accuse Hugh of killing Whirlwind. Miss Hahn *better* keep an eye on her.

Wiping her cheeks, Jas let her head fall back against the tree trunk. She'd love to see the look on Hugh's face when Miss Hahn called and told him that Jas was coming after him.

It was too bad it wouldn't happen. Jas knew she couldn't risk leaving the farm. If the police caught her, she'd never see her grandfather again.

Jas sighed in frustration. She knew that she might as well face it. Just like the sad-eyed horses in the barn, she was stuck at Second Chance Farm.

Chapter 8

Whirr-r-r.

The whining sound of the string trimmer filled Jas's ears as she cut the tall grass around the maple trees in the front yard. It was Friday morning, and for the last four days she'd spent her LOCK time–the time she had to stay close to the monitor–gardening.

I'm really doing a number on this place, Jas thought as she turned off the trimmer and dropped the goggles around her neck. She'd mowed the lawn, shaped the boxwoods, and weeded the beds. She'd even asked Miss Hahn to order a load of mulch, which was being delivered in the afternoon.

Not that this will ever look like High Meadows Farm, Jas reminded herself.

She was walking to the shed, the trimmer hanging off one shoulder, when Mr. Eyler, her probation officer, drove up. Jas didn't stop to greet him, but instead, kept walking toward the house. *He'll catch up,* she said to herself.

They met in the kitchen. Jas sipped a glass of water, her cheeks streaked with sweat, while Mr. Eyler drank a cup of coffee.

"At your trial on Monday, the judge heard only negative things about you." Mr. Eyler set his briefcase on the table and opened it. "Today, we need to come up with at least three goals so that when you go before him in forty-five days he'll see how much progress you've made."

"Forty-one days," Jas corrected.

"Pardon?" Mr. Eyler looked up at her, and Jas met his eyes with a steady gaze.

"I go before the judge in forty-one days," she clarified.

"Right." Mr. Eyler pulled out a file and a pad of paper. "Let's think about three goals you would like to work on during these forty-*one* days. Miss Hahn tells me you've been working in the yard."

"Can't you tell?"

"And that you went to the library Tuesday and checked out some books to read."

"Twenty. I've read six so far."

Jas had checked out lots of books on true crime, detective work, and police procedures. She figured the more she knew about being a detective, the better the chance she had to catch Hugh. But she wasn't about to tell Eyler that.

He raised one pale brow. "You're a fast reader."

"I have a lot of time."

He cleared his throat. "So what do you think you'd like to work on? For example, some kids make remaining drug-free a goal."

"That sounds good for them. But I've always been drug-free," Jas said.

"Oh, right. Well, here's another example that might be more appropriate. Your goal would be to continue following the rules of probation so that you can visit your grandfather a couple times a week. Sound good?"

Jas shot upright in her chair. "You've talked to him? You've seen him? Is he all right? Ms. Tomlinson said she was going to find out where he was, but I haven't heard a word from her."

Mr. Eyler nodded. "Your grandfather's out of the hospital and in The Stanford House, which is an excellent nursing home in town. And he's ready to have visitors." Mr. Eyler smiled. Jas could tell he was genuinely happy to give her the news.

"Thank you." She could feel herself choking up. Quickly, she stood to get another glass of water. "More coffee?"

"No, thank you. So, we can make following probation rules a goal?"

Jas nodded. "Definitely."

"Since you like horses, perhaps one of the goals can be working several hours a day with the animals on the farm. And since you've been doing such a great job in the yard, we could also add more yard and farm work as a goal," said Mr. Eyler.

"Umm, okay," Jas said, frowning.

Great, I bet Miss Hahn put Eyler up to that just so she would get more free labor, she thought. *What a dirty trick.*

"When can I see my grandfather?"

"Hopefully, this Sunday. Is that soon enough?"

"Yes!" She was so excited that she punched the air with her fist.

"I'd like you to think about one more goal." Mr. Eyler thoughtfully tapped his pen on the table. "The judge is going to ask you about what happened the day you assaulted Mr. uh..." He consulted a paper in the file.

"Robicheaux," Jas said.

"That's right. He's going to ask if you understand that you did something wrong so he can judge whether you'll ever do anything like that again."

Jas's gaze dropped to the table.

"You need to put it behind you, Jas."

She nodded. "Of course." Raising her eyes, she

faced him with an expression of such sincere remorse, it was spooky. "I understand why I attacked Mr. Robicheaux. The death of the horse and my grandfather's collapse were overwhelming, and I took it out on Hugh. It was wrong of me."

"I'm glad you've come to grips with it," Mr. Eyler said.

And I'm glad you bought that act, Jas thought. "Perhaps a fourth goal would be learning to control my temper," she continued, the lies rolling smoothly off her tongue. "I know now that I attacked Mr. Robicheaux because I was distraught and lashed out blindly."

"That's an excellent goal. Accepting responsibility for your actions is one of the most important things you can do." He wrote something on his pad. Jas craned her neck, trying to read it. "And how are you and Miss Hahn getting along?" he asked as he closed the file and dropped it in his briefcase.

"Fine."

"That's good."

Really good. Eyler had believed her whole act. Jas sat back with a pleased expression on her face.

☙

Tessa admired Sam from the corner of her

eye. From all angles, Sam Winston was the perfect hunk. Sighing longingly, Tessa shoved her books in her locker. Too bad he didn't even know she was alive.

☜

Jas rolled her eyes as she flopped the book facedown on the quilt. Another story about a girl pining after some guy. How come authors never wrote about missing their grandfathers?

Fluffy the cat started kneading the covers. Jas leaned down and scratched the calico's ears. He was balled in a circle, between her legs. It was nine o'clock Friday night, and they were both in bed. Jas was reading, her riding helmet snug on her head.

Ms. Tomlinson had arrived earlier that night with clothes from the farm. Jas hadn't dared ask her about Old Sam or Phil. But as soon as she'd taken everything to her room, she'd hugged her helmet and riding boots and cried longingly.

A light rap on the door made Jas look up.

"May I come in?"

"Sure." Jas wondered what Miss Hahn wanted. She still couldn't figure the woman out. If she was a spy, she wasn't trying too hard. She never pried or poked around. As far as Jas could tell, the farm and all its dopey animals were the only things she cared about.

When Miss Hahn opened the door, she stared at Jas for a second, a faint smile on her face.

Oops. Jas suddenly realized she was still wearing her riding helmet. Whipping it off, she dropped it on the bed.

"Ms. Tomlinson called. Your Sunday visitation with your grandfather has been approved," Miss Hahn said.

Jas grinned excitedly. "That's great! I can't wait." *I've waited too long as it is.*

"It's set for one o'clock. I'm not sure for how long. That will be up to the nursing home."

"I don't care. I just want to see him." Picking up the book, Jas opened it back to where she had left off, hoping that Miss Hahn would get the hint and leave. Being alone with the woman made her uneasy. Jas was afraid she'd let her guard down or say something she shouldn't.

"One more thing. I'm going to need your help tomorrow."

Jas frowned. "Doing what?"

"Saturday's the auction at Front Royal. I'm one man short. It takes two people to load and haul, and Chase won't be here. You're going to have to come because–"

Because I have to be supervised every second, Jas thought gloomily.

"Because I'm going to need someone who

knows horses. I never know what I'm going to find at the auction."

Jas wondered what she was talking about. In the spring, she'd gone to a horse auction in Kentucky with her grandfather and Phil. The Thoroughbreds had been gorgeous, fetching prices over a million dollars. Obviously, this wasn't that kind of auction.

"Why don't you ask Lucy or one of the other volunteers?" Jas asked.

"They don't have the experience."

"All right, then," Jas reluctantly agreed. She really didn't have a choice. If she refused, Miss Hahn would just mention Jas's obligation to work on the goals Mr. Eyler had written down.

"Good." Miss Hahn gave her a hesitant smile. "Are you enjoying the books you checked out?"

"They're okay. I really like the ones you suggested by James Herriot, the veterinarian in England."

"Chase turned me on to those."

Chase. That was twice she'd heard his name. "We don't have to leave until after lunch," Miss Hahn added.

"Great, that will give me time to spread the mulch." Jas began reading again, hoping that this time Miss Hahn *would* take the hint.

"Well, good night, and I really appreciate

you getting the yard in shape. Everybody's commented on how good it looks."

Jas nodded, her eyes still on the page. When Miss Hahn shut the door, she let out a sigh of relief. Being on constant guard was hard work.

And what really puzzled her was how nice Miss Hahn acted. Then Jas remembered Hugh and his false smile. He'd been able to charm a snake. Miss Hahn was probably just like him.

All week, she'd avoided her foster parent by working in the yard and reading. But tomorrow would have to be different.

Tomorrow, she'd have to spend a whole afternoon with her. With a groan, Jas let the book fall on her face. She wasn't looking forward to it in the least.

Chapter 9

"We have eight hundred and fifty dollars to spend," Miss Hahn shouted above the roar and grind of the oldest pickup truck Jas had ever ridden in.

Eight hundred and fifty dollars? Jas had no idea what kind of horse Miss Hahn expected to buy. Not a Thoroughbred, that was for sure.

Jas was sitting in the front seat, squashed between Miss Hahn and Chase, the person who wasn't supposed to have been coming along. He showed up at the last minute saying he'd decided not to go to the lake with his family after all.

"Since we adopted out Tansey and Gunther, we've got two vacancies," Chase hollered. Behind the truck, the horse trailer creaked and rattled with every twist and bump in the road.

Arms hugging her sides, Jas scrunched herself into a ball so she wouldn't touch any of Chase's body parts. *Oh, why did I wear shorts today?* she thought as she stared at her legs, which looked as white and skinny as noodles.

"And Happy's ready to adopt out, too." Chase leaned forward so he could talk to Miss Hahn. His jeans-clad leg pressed into Jas's thigh. Jas flinched, but continued to stare straight ahead, refusing to look at him—even though he was so close she could smell him.

"We'll have to see what's there," Miss Hahn said. "I just hope it's not another Goldie."

"Goldie?" Jas repeated, grateful to turn her attention to something other than Chase's leg.

"She was a little pony we rescued last month," Miss Hahn explained. "So cute and sweet that you knew at one time she was a little kid's treasured pet. But after we bought her, we soon realized that she was so old and sick that she needed to be put down right on the spot."

Jas wasn't sure she'd heard right. "You mean you rescued a horse just to put it to sleep?"

"We do it all the time," Chase said.

"Our mission is to buy horses who are suffering," Miss Hahn explained. "That means we often have to put them out of their misery."

Jas grimaced. What kind of horses were at this auction? She hoped none like Ruffles.

The truck hit a pothole, and Jas clutched her stomach. The swaying and bouncing, the smell of sweat, and the talk about killing horses were beginning to make her carsick.

"Are you all right?" Chase asked. He was tilted forward, his head turned toward her. "You're as white as a sheet."

Jas realized he was being nice. Still, she couldn't forget what a creep he'd been on Monday. "Don't worry," she muttered. "I promise I won't barf again."

"That's *not* why I was worrying," he muttered right back. "But now that you mention it, please don't."

Reaching forward, he flipped on the radio and searched for a good song.

Crossing her arms, Jas glared out the windshield as a country singer crooned, *"My baby left me flat, takin' my heart and my cat."*

Miss Hahn made a noise of disgust, turned down the volume, then switched the station to classical music. Chase protested.

"When you're old enough to drive, you can pick the station," she told him.

Fifteen minutes later, they pulled into the county fairgrounds, where the auction was being held. The parking lot was filled with horse trailers, vans, and a half-dozen two-tiered tractor-trailers. "The killer buyers are in full force today," Miss Hahn said grimly as they passed a tractor-trailer half filled with horses.

"Killer buyers?" Jas repeated.

"That's right," said Miss Hahn.

They parked under a lone tree. Jas slid across the seat while Chase held the door. Her stomach was a bit upset from the ride. She didn't want to be here, and for once it didn't have anything to do with Miss Hahn or Chase.

After cracking the windows, Miss Hahn locked the truck. "Let's tour the pens first," she said to Chase. "And see what we've got."

"Right." Chase glanced at Jas, who stood woodenly by the truck door. For a second, she met his gaze. His eyes were so blue, they matched the cloudless sky.

Although she didn't want to, Jas couldn't help but wonder what Chase was thinking when he looked at her. An angry horse snob with pale thighs? Or maybe someone he thought was too scared to find out what this auction was all about? Or maybe an attractive young... Jas stopped to clear her head.

"You coming?" he asked.

"No, it's all right. I think I'll stay here," she said. "I brought a book." She held it up, blushing when she remembered that a girl and boy were kissing on the cover. Quickly, she flipped it around.

"Suit yourself," he muttered as he headed across the grass toward a low building.

Miss Hahn came around the front of the truck. "Don't mind him, Jas. He pretends he can handle it, but it's hard for him, too. It's hard for all of us."

"Then why do you do it?"

Miss Hahn shook her head. She'd worn a baseball cap with a logo that read: ALL GOD'S CREATURES HAVE A PLACE IN HEAVEN.

"Because someone has to. But we aren't making that much of a dent. About eighty percent of the horses at this auction will be bought by the killers. We obviously can't save them all."

Jas had heard enough. Pressing the book against her chest, she hurried over to a tree. "I'll just stay here and read," she said, plopping down Indian-style with her back against the tree.

Miss Hahn studied her.

"Don't worry. I'll be here when you get back," Jas assured her.

"I know. We'll try not to be too long," Miss Hahn said, smiling. Then she left, striding after Chase with her swinging gait. *Like a pirate with a peg leg,* Jas decided, wondering if she'd injured it riding.

Opening the book, Jas tried to read about lovesick Tessa and hunky Sam, but her mind drifted every time a horse whinnied or a truck started up. Whenever a horse was loaded on one of the huge tractor-trailers, the echo of hooves on the wooden ramp made Jas's heart ache.

She knew about the killer buyers. They bought loads of horses and hauled them to slaughterhouses. The meat was then shipped to Europe and Japan, where horse steaks are considered a delicacy.

A man wearing a cowboy hat, his cheek bulging with chewing tobacco, walked by leading a horse. Jas watched the horse shuffle past, his head hanging so low that his bottom lip grazed the tips of the high grass.

He was a big horse, over sixteen-three hands. Jas could tell that he had once been muscular, too. Jas thought he might be a Thoroughbred or a Warmblood, though it was hard to tell since his body was so gaunt, his coat sprinkled with orange hair, his gait awkward because of stiffness in his hind end.

As she continued to watch the horse pass, it dawned on Jas what was wrong with him. Last spring, Pocomo Pete, one of Hugh's top field hunters, had started looking just like this one. At first, Hugh's vet had been baffled. But after many tests, the vet figured out what was wrong. And Jas had spent so many hours with Pocomo and the vet that she'd recognize the same symptoms anywhere.

Closing her book, she jumped to her feet. *What's going to happen to this horse?* she thought. Her stomach began to tighten at the possibilities.

Leaving her book by the tree, Jas hurried after the man and the horse. They disappeared through the entrance to the auction. *"Eighty percent of the horses at this auction will be bought by the killers."* Miss Hahn's statement echoed in Jas's head. When she reached the building, she looked inside.

People and horses were everywhere. She could hear the singsong voice of the auctioneer, and when she glanced to the left, she saw bleachers half hidden by a high wall. Beyond the wall was a small arena. She could just see the head of a horse as someone led it in front of the bidders.

To her left and right were temporary stalls. At the end of the aisle, a ceiling-tall door opened to the outside, where she spotted corrals filled with horses, burros, and ponies.

The cowboy and the horse were nowhere in sight. Jas walked down the aisle, peering into the stalls. Several held two or more horses packed together like sardines. They all had numbers stuck to their rumps.

Crossing the aisle, she started up the other side. Since the place was spilling over with animals, she had no idea why she was so interested in this one horse. Maybe it was because she knew what was wrong with him. She knew he could be treated. She knew she could help. It had taken Pocomo Pete only two weeks to change from a depressed, sore-legged, orange-coated horse to his glossy, feisty old self. Pocomo was given a second chance. Unless she did something, this horse wouldn't have one.

As Jas passed the third stall, she saw him. He was standing in the darkest corner, facing away from her, his head in the shadows.

Hiding, Jas thought. *Just like me.*

Opening the door, she stepped inside. The horse turned his head to look at her. His ears drooped. His expression was listless. Like Pocomo Pete, he had given up.

"Hey." Jas approached him with her hand outstretched. He didn't move. She scratched his forehead and under his mane. On his face, he had a strip of white ending in a dot on his nose, as if someone had painted an exclamation point. She thought he was chestnut, though his coat was so dull it was hard to tell.

But his front legs were straight and strong with good bone, and his hooves were solid, even though he wasn't shod. Bending, Jas saw old nail holes in both the front and hind hooves. It hadn't been that long since he'd worn shoes.

Stepping back, she stared at him. What was his story? Had he once been someone's treasured pet, like Goldie?

Stretching out his neck, the horse snuffled the front of Jas's T-shirt. For just an instant, his eyes brightened, and Jas saw a trace of the elegant horse he had once been.

"Hey! What are you doing in that stall?" a voice barked.

Startled, Jas spun around. The cowboy stood in the doorway, his hands on his hips.

"I–I like your horse," she stammered.

"Good." Striding over, he slapped a number on the horse's rump. "Then you can bid on him. 'Cause he's going in next."

Chapter 10

"Next?" Jas yelled. Reaching up, she laced her fingers into the horse's coarse mane. "You can't let him go to the killers."

"Why not?" the cowboy said as he spat in the dirt. "At a dollar a pound, this big guy will bring me some real good money."

"But I know what's wrong with him," Jas protested. "He can be cured."

The cowboy snorted. "Cured? That's a hoot. Like I'm going to pay some doctor big bucks to fix an old nag who'll never amount to anything."

Jas caught her breath when she heard his words. She couldn't believe she had said the same thing to Chase.

"Besides, who cares what's wrong with him? All I'm interested in is the quick money," the cowboy said as he leaned forward. He wasn't that old, Jas realized, probably in his early twenties. But his teeth were stained and his breath stunk. "So, little honey, I suggest if you want him, you better rustle up the money."

She shrank away from him. "I don't have any money."

Throwing his head back, he let out a guffaw. "I get it, you're one of them bleeding heart animal fanatics." He eyed her up and down. "If you weren't so cute, I'd kick you out pronto. But, maybe, if you *really* like this horse..." His voice trailed off and he winked.

Jas narrowed her eyes. She'd met a dozen jerks like him at the center. "I like your *horse,* not *you.* So, if you'll excuse me."

She started to push around him, but he stepped in her path and blocked her. Usually, when she confronted the big mouths at the center, they backed off. But this guy wasn't a kid, and it scared her.

"Jas? What are you doing in there?" Jas had never been so relieved to hear a familiar voice—even if it was Chase's.

"Excuse me," she repeated through clenched teeth. "I have to leave."

Grinning, the cowboy shrugged, then stepped aside. "Okay. But you don't know what you're missing."

Eyes downcast, Jas rushed out the door, brushed past Chase, and headed down the aisle.

"Hey." Chase fell into step beside her. "What

were you doing in a stall with Reaves?"

"You know that creep? He's one of your friends?" Jas demanded.

"Not even close." He caught her arm and stopped her from walking away. "Reaves is a crook. You scared the pants off me when I saw you in there."

Jas's eyes brimmed with tears. "I'm sorry. He scared the pants off me, too," she admitted as her tears spilled over. For a second, they stood in the middle of the aisle, Jas silently crying, Chase standing close with his hand on her arm as horses and people filed past.

"Oh, this is so stupid," Jas finally mumbled, wiping her cheeks with her fingers. "It's not like I haven't met jerks before."

Chase dropped his hand. "I hope you don't mean me. Though I guess the way I've been acting lately, I probably qualify." He sounded so glum that Jas choked out a laugh.

Chase frowned. "What's so funny?"

"Nothing. Thanks for coming to my rescue," she said lightly, as if she was joking. When she glanced at him, he was smiling at her. Embarrassed, she looked down at her tennis shoes. *You can't let yourself like this guy,* she told herself. *It's too risky.*

"So what *were* you doing in the stall with

Reaves?" he asked.

"I wasn't in the stall with *him*. I was with his horse." Straightening, she looked back at the stall. The door was shut, as if the cowboy had left. Did he take the horse into the arena? "Oh, no, I hope he's not being auctioned off already." Without a second's thought, Jas ran back to the stall. The big horse stood in the corner, his head still hidden in the shadows.

Jas hooked her fingers through the wire. Beside her, Chase tipped back his cap and squinted into the stall. "Okay, it's a horse," he acknowledged.

"A sick horse," Jas corrected.

Chase looked down at her. "Lots of horses at the auction are sick."

"But this horse can be fixed!"

Shaking his head in disbelief, Chase leaned one shoulder against the stall wall. "Most of them can be fixed, unless they're really old or so far gone that the only humane thing is to put them to sleep. That one in there's no different."

"But he *is* different!" Jas protested. "He's probably a Warmblood or Thoroughbred, and he's got great bone and confirmation. With some TLC, he'd make somebody a hunter or dressage–"

Jerking upright, Chase smacked the wooden wall with his palm. "There you go again, talking about stuff that doesn't mean a thing. Every horse at this auction is worth saving even if it will never win a ribbon."

Jas propped her hands on her hips. "That's so narrow-minded! You could save that horse in there, fix him up, resell him for big bucks, and then use the money to save ten Goldies."

"We don't sell the horses for profit!" he argued right back. "We adopt them out and make sure they go to homes where the people love them for what they are and not because they can jump a fence or run around a barrel."

He jerked his thumb toward the horse in the stall. "That horse is in there because someone decided that since he couldn't perform some award-winning feat, he wasn't valuable any-more. He's being sold for meat because some stuck-up horse snob like *you* owned him!"

Blue eyes flashing, Chase yanked his cap brim low, then spun around and stormed down the aisle.

Openmouthed, Jas stared after him. *You're wrong!* she wanted to shout. Only suddenly, hor-ribly, she realized he wasn't. Even though every inch of her loved horses, after living at High Meadows Farm for five years, where only the perfect horses were raised and kept, she had turned into another Hugh Robicheaux.

With a groan, Jas sank back against the stall wall. Chase was right. She *was* a horse snob.

"Jas? What's going on?" Miss Hahn came up, a concerned look on her face. "Chase just barreled past me without saying a word."

Jas exhaled loudly. "Nothing."

Miss Hahn cocked one brow. "I thought you were waiting outside for us?"

"I was. But I followed this horse inside." Turning slowly, Jas looked back into the stall. The big horse hadn't moved. Not a switch of his tail, not a flicker of his ear.

Miss Hahn turned and looked in, too. "Nice," she commented.

Jas twisted to face her. "You think so?"

She nodded. "I watched Reaves bring him in. Long stride, balanced. Handsome despite his condition. I often see horses like this when I come here. Lots of perfectly healthy Thoroughbreds off the track are sold to the killers simply because they weren't fast enough."

"But why don't their owners sell them to someone who will turn them into a hunter or pleasure horse?" Jas asked.

"Too much trouble. And with prices for horse meat so high, they can get just as much money here, and faster."

"That doesn't make sense."

"It does if all you're interested in is money." Suddenly Jas remembered conversations she'd overheard between Hugh and other horse owners.

"The mare's a producer of quality foals. She's a daughter of a Grand Prix winner whose off-spring is selling for $250,000. Buy her, and you're making an investment for life."

He was exactly the kind of owner Miss Hahn was talking about. And maybe that's why he'd killed Whirlwind. Because she was no longer valuable for some reason.

Frowning, Jas studied Miss Hahn out of the corner of her eye. The woman didn't make sense to her. If Miss Hahn was telling the truth, she was the total opposite of horse owners like Hugh. But how could someone so different from Hugh be working with him?

"I'd love to buy every one of them," Miss Hahn continued wistfully. "With a couple of months' retraining, most of them could turn into a great mount for some kid who can't afford the sky-high prices that decent horses are going for these days. Only the farm doesn't have the facilities or someone who's a good enough rider."

"Why can't you work with them? You're a good rider," Jas said, quickly adding, "Uh, I sort of saw those pictures on your dresser."

"That was a long time and several injuries ago," Miss Hahn explained, with a wry glance at her leg.

Jas bit a fingernail, the spark of an idea forming in her brain. Miss Hahn definitely had a different perspective than the high and mighty Chase. Just maybe Jas could convince her to buy...

Jas caught herself. What was she doing? She didn't want to have anything to do with a woman who was a friend of Hugh's. But if she didn't do something right now, the horse in the shadows would be sold for meat.

"Well, that's too bad you don't have the facilities," Jas said with an exaggerated sigh. "That big guy in there would be perfect for retraining. Especially since I know what's wrong with him."

"You do?"

"Yeah, I used to know this horse called Pocomo Pete. His condition was caused by a problem in the thyroid gland. The vet that treated him explained to me that the thyroid controls the cells in the body. I didn't understand exactly, but in horses, when it doesn't work right, it causes weight loss, depression, an orange-colored coat, and stiffness—just like that horse in there's got."

Miss Hahn was studying her thoughtfully.

"You really do know a lot about horses, don't you?"

"And the thing is, the condition can easily be cured," Jas rushed on. "With a special supplement, there's no reason that horse can't be perfectly healthy again in a few weeks!"

For a second, Miss Hahn didn't say anything. Jas crossed her fingers as the woman turned and examined the horse.

"Reaves will expect about nine hundred dollars for this one," Miss Hahn said. "And we don't have that much. But, the number on the horse's rump shows he won't be auctioned off until the end of the day, which gives us an advantage."

"How?"

"By the end of the sale, the killers' tractor-trailers are pretty full. And this horse is a big one. He'll be hard to cram into a packed trailer."

Miss Hahn tapped her lip as if thinking hard. "And Reaves knows that, which means if someone offered him cash *now*..."

"You mean you're going to try and buy the horse?" Jas asked excitedly.

"Only on one condition." Miss Hahn looked at Jas with a very serious expression.

"What?" asked Jas warily. She should have known. This was where Miss Hahn was going to show her true colors. This was where she was going to demand that Jas forget all about Whirlwind and leave Hugh alone.

"He's *your* project. You take care of him. You retrain him."

Jas stared at her, totally taken aback. "Sure," she blurted.

"Then come on." Miss Hahn said, sounding like a kid about to get into trouble. "Let's go buy a horse."

Chapter 11

Sunday morning, the day after the auction, Jas finally got to see her grandfather. He was sitting in a wheelchair in front of the dayroom window, his back toward her. Jas would have recognized him anywhere, even though he was thinner and shorter.

"Grandfather!" Rushing over, Jas sank to her knees and buried her face in his stomach so he wouldn't see her tears.

His right hand pressed against her head, and she could feel his fingers tremble. "Jas-s." He slurred her name.

Looking up, Jas could see that his mouth was crooked. One side of it was tilting up in a smile, while the other was frozen in a straight line. "I'm so glad to see you, Grandfather. I missed you so much."

He nodded, tears filling his own eyes. "Me too."

"How have you been?" Sitting back on her

heels, Jas studied him. "Are they taking good care of you?"

He nodded, drool trickling from the side of his mouth. His hair was sticking up in gray wisps, and his eyes were cloudy. Jas wanted to cry out loud at the change in him. A month ago, even at the age of sixty-eight, he'd been strong enough to lift two bales of hay.

"I'm etter every ay," he said, patting her shoulder with his right hand. His other hand lay by his side, the fingers curled loosely. Ducking his head, he gestured toward a straight-backed chair under the picture window. "Sit."

When Jas went to get the chair, she looked around the dayroom. It was decorated in pastels. The sun streamed through the huge window. Games, magazines, and books were strewn on several tables. Only no one was reading or playing. One woman watched TV, her head flopped to the side, while several other patients shuffled randomly across the shiny tile floor.

"Your doctor's going to talk to me after our visit," Jas said, setting the chair in front of him. "Miss Hahn, my foster parent, brought me today. She'll bring me back on Wednesday, too. I tried to see you before, but the visit had to be written into my schedule and I had to obey all these rules and..."

Raising a thin, blue-veined hand, Grandfather stroked Jas's hair.

She caught his hand and held it to her cheek. "Oh, Grandfather, nothing is right." Jas struggled with what to say.

"I know." His eyes watered. "Il came to ee me."

"What?" Jas asked, not sure what he was saying.

"Il arks."

"*Phil* came to see you."

"Ee told me everything."

Jas pressed his palm hard against her cheek. "Did he tell you that I attacked Hugh and that I'm on probation? I can't ever go to High Meadows again."

"Good! I on't ant you ever on at farm again."

Twisting his hand, he grasped Jas's fingers and squeezed them tightly, and she could feel the conviction of his words.

"Why don't you want me on the farm again?"

"Ecause Hugh is..." He took a shuddering breath. "E-vil." He pronounced the words with such effort that Jas could feel his arm shake. *Grandfather knew.*

"What else did Phil tell you?"

"Ee said ee thinks Hugh killed Irlwind."

"Yes! I think he killed Whirlwind, too. But why, Grandfather? Does Phil know?"

He shook his head.

"Is he going to find out?"

He shook his head again. "Worried about is ob."

"He doesn't want to lose his job. I understand." Phil had two teenage sons in college and a daughter ready to graduate from high school. Hugh paid him a good salary. If he was fired, he'd have to start all over.

"Well, *I'm* going to find out," Jas stated. "I have nothing to lose. Except you." Jas clamped both hands around his, suddenly afraid to let go.

Her grandfather swung his head violently. "Oo stay away from Hugh!"

"I won't go near him. Promise. But if you help me, we can figure out why Hugh killed Whirlwind. You must have an idea, Grandfather."

"Orget about Hugh. As oon as I am well, we'll leave Stanford." Struggling to lean forward, he drew in a ragged breath.

"All right," Jas agreed quickly. "Now calm down. I don't want you to hurt yourself."

He slumped back in the wheelchair, his breathing ragged. Jas jumped up, searching anxiously for a nurse. Miss Hahn stood in the doorway.

Jas's heart fell to her knees. How long had she been there? Had she heard what they were saying about Hugh?

"I'm not ready to go yet," Jas said, her voice quivering with anger.

"That's fine," Miss Hahn said. "The doctor wants to see us both. I'll tell her it will be a few more minutes."

Arms rigid by her sides, Jas watched her leave. Her grandfather tugged on her hand. "Jas-s-s," he said. "You eed to orget about Irlwind."

"But I can't," Jas declared. "I can't forget about Hugh, either. Too much has happened. I'm just now realizing what kind of person he is."

Her grandfather made such a strange sound that Jas looked down at him. One side of his mouth was tilted almost wickedly, and she could see a trace of his crafty old self.

She grinned back at him. "I knew you'd understand. I knew you'd help. Especially since he accused *you* of putting the yew in the paddock. The snake." For a second, the thought of what Hugh had done made her tremble with anger; then she turned her attention back to her grandfather. "Now we need to get you well. Is there anything I can do?"

He nodded. "Alk to Dr. Anvers."

"Dr. Anvers? But I thought your doctor here was named Bindera?"

"It is. I ant you to alk to Anvers."

"Dr. Danvers! You mean Hugh's vet?" Jas's eyes widened.

"Ee ad to ex-am-ine Irlwind after she d-ied," her grandfather continued, his voice insistent.

"Why would he examine Whirlwind if she was dead?" Jas asked, not understanding.

"Insurance."

Jas's mouth dropped open. *Of course! Insurance!* Why hadn't she thought of that? Hugh insured all his horses against accidental death. "Do you think he killed her for the insurance money?"

Grandfather shrugged, although only one shoulder was able to move. She touched his cheek. His face was pale with exhaustion.

"Hey, that's enough for today. I don't want to wear you out completely," she said, patting his arm. Someone had dressed him in a short-sleeved dress shirt and polyester slacks. Ever since she could remember, he'd worn jeans hitched up with suspenders and a long-sleeved denim shirt.

"I need to bring you some work clothes," she said. "That'll make you feel more like your old self."

He nodded in agreement. "Tell me ow you are."

"I'm okay. Miss Hahn, my foster parent, runs this farm for rescued horses," she said, choosing her words carefully. She didn't want to scare her grandfather with her suspicions about Miss Hahn and Hugh. "Yesterday, we went to a killer auction and bought a horse. I'm supposed to work with him as part of my probation agreement."

Jas's voice rose in excitement as she talked about the big horse. "I named him Shadow, because he likes to hide in dark corners. You wouldn't believe what a mess he is, nothing like Whirlwind or Hugh's other horses."

She told her grandfather about spotting Shadow and realizing he had the same illness as Pocomo Pete. Then she went on to tell him how the horse was so weak that they practically had to lift him into the trailer.

"Chase, a boy who works at the farm, he and I had to link hands behind Shadow's hindquarters and push him into the trailer while Miss Hahn pulled. We finally got him back to the farm, and tomorrow Miss Hahn's vet will be in to examine him and–"

"Miss Schuler?" a voice cut in.

Jas turned. A nurse with a friendly smile had come up beside Grandfather's wheelchair. "Dr. Bindera would like to speak to you now. Besides, it's time for your grandfather's nap."

"Oh, right." Jas glanced back at her grandfather. His eyelids were drooping. "I think I wore him out."

"No, you relieved his anxiety. He's been very worried about you. And now that he's seen you, I think he'll be able to relax and concentrate on his therapy. We need to get him up and walking."

Jas stood up. Grandfather's chin had dropped to his chest and he was snoring softly. She touched his hand one last time, then followed the nurse into the hall.

Jas tensed up when she saw Miss Hahn sitting in the office with Dr. Bindera.

On the drive over, Miss Hahn had asked Jas if she could listen in on the conversation with the doctor, explaining that she'd gone through the same thing with her mother. Jas hesitantly answered yes. She might be able to take care of herself, but she knew she couldn't take care of her grandfather. She didn't know the first thing about nursing homes or strokes.

But after catching Miss Hahn listening in on her conversation with her grandfather, Jas wasn't sure if she wanted anything from this woman.

"Your grandfather is doing well, Miss Schuler," Dr. Bindera, a plump woman with pitch-black hair, said, gesturing to a chair. "He's very determined, and his previous strength and good health have given him an edge in recovery. Plus, his mind was not affected by the stroke, so he was lucky."

"Good." Jas sat down, her hands clasped in her lap. "How long will he have to stay here?"

"That's hard to say. It depends on his progress. His left side suffered quite a bit of paralysis. Since he is right-handed it won't affect him quite as much. We will continue working daily on his speech and strength."

"I guess that's good news." Jas hoped the doctor was being straightforward with her. If she was, then it sounded as if Grandfather was getting excellent care. Hugh had kept his end of the deal. When they left the nursing home five minutes later, Miss Hahn asked, "Did you have a nice visit with your grandfather?"

"You should know," Jas retorted.

Miss Hahn stopped in the middle of the parking lot. "Pardon me?" she asked.

Jas shot her an angry look. She couldn't believe the woman was going to pretend she hadn't been eavesdropping. "Never mind." Striding ahead, Jas yanked open the car door and slid into the seat. She wasn't going to say another word. She wasn't going to give Miss Hahn anything more to tell Hugh.

"Dr. Bindera seemed very competent," Miss Hahn said a few minutes later as she started the car. "Speaking of doctors, Dr. Danvers will be at the farm tomorrow afternoon to check Shadow."

"Dr. *Danvers?*" Jas repeated, turning to face her.

"Yes, he's the farm's veterinarian. He donates quite a bit of his time."

Jas's heart thumped excitedly. She couldn't believe her luck.

"Shadow will have to stay in quarantine until Dr. Danvers gives him a clean bill of health," Miss Hahn went on.

But Jas wasn't listening. She was thinking about Dr. Danvers. She had been wondering how she was going to contact the vet. Calling him up to ask him questions about Whirlwind would seem too suspicious.

But now he was coming to Second Chance Farm, and all Jas had to do was just *happen* to mention Whirlwind. That would definitely appear pretty normal.

Jas wanted to grin, but she didn't dare. Miss Hahn might figure something was up. This could just be the break she needed to find out why Hugh had killed Whirlwind.

Chapter 12

"You were right, Jas," Dr. Danvers said as he capped the vial of blood and stuck it in the pocket of his coveralls. "This horse acts just like Pocomo Pete's twin. The blood tests will tell us for sure if he has a thyroid condition. Until then, I'm starting him on the treatment anyways."

"Great." Jas stroked Shadow's neck. He hadn't moved during the entire examination, even when Danvers pushed the needle into his neck. In fact, he was so listless that Jas was beginning to worry. Even a crisp, sweet-smelling section of alfalfa hay hadn't tempted his appetite.

"How old is he?" Jas asked. At the auction, Miss Hahn had checked his teeth and guessed his age at twelve.

"About twelve or thirteen. He's no spring chicken, but definitely young enough to bounce back."

Unsnapping the lead line from Shadow's halter, Jas followed Danvers out of the stall, almost running over Chase, who'd been hovering in the aisle. All afternoon, he'd hung around the vet, just like Tilly would tag after Miss Hahn.

Dr. Danvers walked down to Ruffles's stall, Chase trotting beside him. "So what's wrong with the big guy?" he asked.

"We'll know when the blood test comes back. It will be determined by how much of the hormone thyroxin is present in the bloodstream," Danvers explained to Chase, who bobbed his head as he hung on every word.

Opening the stall door, Danvers went in to check on Ruffles. Jas couldn't believe the change in the Morgan horse in just one week. His ears pricked eagerly when someone came in the stall, and his ribs didn't stick out quite so much.

"Looks good," Danvers said as he inspected the wound on the Morgan horse's back. "Healed completely. Tomorrow, you can start turning him out for about an hour each day. Alone, of course."

"All right!" Chase slapped Ruffles fondly on the neck.

Oh, go away, Chase, Jas fumed to herself, impatient to talk to Danvers alone.

"How about corn oil in Shadow's grain?" Jas asked when the vet left the stall.

Dr. Danvers nodded. "Couldn't hurt. He needs the extra fat, that's for sure."

"Maybe we could try him on some grass," Chase suggested. "That might get him to eat."

"Good idea!" Jas thrust the lead line in his hand. "Why don't you turn him out in one of the paddocks? It's almost six, so it's cool enough."

Chase cocked one brow.

"Please-se," Jas pleaded.

"All right." When Chase went into the stall to get Shadow, Jas hurried after Danvers, who was headed to his truck parked outside the barn.

"Dr. Danvers," Jas puffed as she caught up with him.

Turning, he handed her a bottle filled with some sort of powder. "Two scoops in his grain. The corn oil might help mask the taste."

"Thanks."

"Shadow should thank *you*," Danvers said as he wrote the horse's name on a piece of paper. "For saving him from the killers."

"For that, he needs to thank Miss Hahn."

At the mention of her name, Danvers's eyes slid to the office. "Yes, Diane's pretty remarkable," he said, a strangely soft expression on his weather-beaten face.

Jas's eyes widened, and she followed his gaze toward the office. Did Danvers have a crush on Miss Hahn?

She glanced back at the vet. They *were* about

the same age. And neither was married…

Nah. Jas quickly dismissed the idea. The two were too old to be romantic, and Miss Hahn and her baggy overalls were hardly an irresistible sight. "Dr. Danvers." Jas went around to the back of the truck, realizing she'd better hurry if she was going to ask him about Whirlwind. Not only was he ready to leave, but at six she had to be back in the house for lockdown. "Can I ask you some questions…" Jas hesitated, then blurted out, "about Whirlwind?"

"Ummm." He paused for a second. "I would have been surprised if you hadn't," he finally said. "I know her death was hard on everybody."

"Yes," Jas whispered as the memory of the whole awful afternoon came rushing back. She pressed her fingers to her eyelids, hoping to shut out the image of Whirlwind lying dead in the paddock.

Dr. Danvers gave her his full attention. "What did you want to ask me?"

Jas dropped her hands. "Did the yew kill her?"

"Yes. The blood test confirmed it, though technically it was the convulsions caused by ingesting the plant that killed her. Her intestines twisted and…"

Jas held up both hands. "Please stop." Her

eyes blurred. "I don't want to hear how she suffered."

Danvers put a comforting arm around her shoulder. "I'm sorry, Jas. I'm sorry for everything."

She nodded silently. He handed her a tissue from the truck, and she blew her nose.

"How are the foals?" she asked when she finally collected herself. "And how's Old Sam? Is his arthritis acting up? I haven't been back to the farm. Well, I guess you already knew that," she added, feeling a rush of embarrassment.

He must know everything, she realized. Hugh had probably told him the whole story.

Dropping his arm from her shoulder, Danvers turned away. "I don't know, Jas. I haven't been back to the farm, either."

"Why not?"

"Hugh's using a new vet."

Jas caught her breath. That didn't make sense. Danvers was the best in the area. "Why?"

"Well, part of it's my fault. I've just been so busy. And you know, Hugh, he likes VIP treatment." He smiled at Jas, but she thought it seemed forced. "If Hugh or Phil calls, the new vet drops everything and rushes out there. Then Hugh wanted me to put Sam to sleep, and I refused."

"Put Sam to sleep!" Jas gasped. "But he can't. Sam's Grandfather's dog."

"That's what I told him. Hugh said if I wasn't going to do it, he'd get a vet who would."

He started to pile the boxes of worm medicine in Jas's arms. "Diane said she needed to worm five horses."

As if in a trance, Jas hugged the boxes. "Was there any other reason why you left?"

Danvers leveled a stern gaze at her. "I'm sorry, Jas. I can't discuss my business with you." Closing the cab of the truck, he walked around to the passenger side.

"Why? Because I'm just a kid?" Jas jogged after him. "Or because you know something about Whirlwind's death!"

Opening the truck door, Danvers slid into the front seat, then turned to face her. "I signed the death certificate stating Whirlwind died from complications of poisoning. I wasn't there when she died, so I don't know what else might have happened."

"But you don't believe Hugh's story about Grandfather accidentally putting the yew in Whirlwind's paddock, do you?" Jas insisted.

"Let's just say I think your grandfather is one of the finest men I know."

Jas caught the door handle so he couldn't

close it. "Then tell me one more thing," she pressed. "If Grandfather didn't put the yew in there, who did?"

Danvers's bushy brows dipped in a frown. "That's enough, Jas. I already told you I wasn't discussing this with you, which means I'm certainly *not* going to go around accusing anyone." He pointed a finger at her. "And neither should you," he added sternly as he turned and started the truck.

Jas stepped back, and he slammed the door shut. When he wheeled the truck around, she noticed Miss Hahn standing in the office doorway, watching. Miss Hahn waved at Danvers when the truck drove past, then looked curiously at Jas before ducking back into the office.

Spying again, Jas thought. At least she was too far away to hear what they had said.

When the truck disappeared from sight, Jas exhaled in frustration. She hadn't learned anything from their conversation? She knew exactly what she'd already known–that Grandfather hadn't killed Whirlwind.

Scuffing the toes of her sneakers in the dirt, she walked slowly back to the barn. She stuck the worm medicine on the shelf in the feed room, then went out to the paddock. Shadow was cropping indifferently at the grass, ignoring the chickens who milled around his legs eating crickets.

Jas couldn't believe the horse didn't mind the brainless birds. Whirlwind would have pranced and snorted in mock fright. Then, with a toss of her head, she would have playfully chased the squawking things from the paddock.

Sighing, Jas crossed her arms on the top of the board fence and propped her chin on her wrists. Maybe she made a big mistake saying she'd work with Shadow. He might never turn into anything but a plodding old school horse.

But, according to Chase, a plodding old school horse was just as valuable as the winner of the Triple Crown.

Jas watched as Shadow ambled over to a patch of weeds. He tore at a flowered stalk, then with a wiggle of his lips, spit it right out.

Suddenly, Jas smacked her forehead with her palm. Why hadn't she thought of it before!

Whirlwind was fed the finest, sweetest feed available. Why would she eat something as nasty as yew?

She wouldn't. Not unless she'd been really hungry.

But how could Whirlwind have possibly been hungry? Jas knew that she had fed her the night and morning before.

But then it all started to make sense. Phil and Grandfather had left for two days to take the stock trailer to Maryland to pick up cattle. That same night, Jas had rushed through the horse feeding at High Meadows because she'd had other horses to ride at a nearby farm for one of Hugh's clients. Then, the next morning, she'd had to catch the bus early for school. So on the morning she left for school, Hugh had been the only one at the farm.

Jas bit her teeth into the skin of her wrist.

Hugh had set the whole thing up! He got rid of her, Phil, and Grandfather so that he could be alone in the barn. So that he could remove Whirlwind's feed both times. Now she knew why Whirlwind was hungry enough to eat yew.

Now she knew how Hugh had killed her.

Chapter 13

"You hungry, Jas?"

Startled, she quickly spun around.

"The way you were chewing on your arm, I figured you needed a snack," Chase said, smiling.

"Nope," said Jas calmly, even though she was still bursting with thoughts about Hugh.

Chase tapped the face of his watch. "It's almost six, you know."

"Oh, shoot. I've got to get to the house for lockdown." Immediately, Jas took off running.

"Hey, Cinderella!" Chase hollered after her. "You dropped a sneaker!"

Jas raced across the barnyard, scattering the geese. When she reached the kitchen, she could hear the cuckoo clock cuckooing six o'clock.

She just made it.

Miss Hahn was working at the counter, slicing a cantaloupe. Beside her, something was sputtering and popping around in a lidded frying pan. "I was just about to holler for you,"

Miss Hahn said.

Jas gasped for breath, holding her side. "No need. I made it."

"Chase is going to stay for dinner," Miss Hahn added. "So I'm actually cooking a decent meal for once. Fried chicken. It'll be ready in about half an hour."

Jas straightened and rubbed the stitch under her rib. "Doesn't Chase have a home? On Saturday night, we all stopped for burgers on the way back from the auction, and last night he ate that takeout pizza with us in front of the TV," Jas said, protesting.

"His folks are still at the lake," Miss Hahn explained.

Jas feigned disgust when she heard the screen door slam and Chase sauntered into the kitchen. Reaching around Miss Hahn, he grabbed a slice of cantaloupe and took a big bite.

"Wash first, please," Miss Hahn scolded.

"Really," Jas muttered as juice dribbled down his chin. "You're such a slob."

Chase pointed at her stained T-shirt. "And what about you?"

"Oh, shut up," replied Jas. "Miss Hahn, may I use the phone? I forgot to ask Dr. Danvers some-thing about, uh, Shadow."

"Sure. You better call him at home, though.

He'll probably be there for dinner before going off to the office or on another call. That man works night and day."

Jas hurried into the living room and plopped down on the sofa next to Furry. Both of Dr. Danvers's numbers were on the list of emergency numbers by the phone.

As Jas dialed, Chase came and stood in the doorway, slouched against the frame. He studied her as he ate another slice of cantaloupe. She shot him a "get lost" look that he totally ignored. Jas couldn't decide if he was too dense or too rude. When Danvers answered, she turned her back on Chase and lowered her voice. "Hi, Dr. Danvers, I'm sorry if I'm interrupting dinner, but I need to ask you a couple more questions."

"Go ahead, Jas. I was just about to stick one of those frozen things in the microwave."

"Really? Well, actually, the first question I wanted to ask is, Would you like to come over for dinner tonight? You left so quickly, Miss Hahn didn't get the chance to ask you."

"Oh?" There was a pause. Jas couldn't believe she'd invited him to dinner, but then again, maybe she'd have more of a chance to quiz him about Whirlwind.

"Fried chicken," she said enticingly.

"Sure. I'd love to."

"The other question is about Whirlwind's autopsy. Did she have anything else wrong with her?"

This time there was a long pause as if Danvers was measuring his words. "No. She appeared very healthy other than the complications from the poison."

"Last question—did she have anything in her stomach besides the yew?"

"Her stomach was pretty empty."

Jas swallowed hard. She was right. "Thank you. I just wondered why she ate the yew in the first place. So we'll see you in fifteen minutes?"

"Yup. And Jas, no more questions about Whirlwind. Okay?"

Jas crossed her fingers. "Okay." As she hung up the phone, her mind raced. Whirlwind *had* been hungry. And yew was so toxic that eating only a small amount would have caused her death.

"What was that all about?" Chase asked.

Jas stiffened. Had he been listening the whole time?

"I invited Dr. Danvers over for dinner," Jas said. "Do you think Miss Hahn will mind?"

"No. She's had the hots for him for ages." Shoving his hands in his pockets, he strolled over to the sofa with a curious gaze.

Jas stared at him. *Something is different about him. But what is it?*

His baseball cap! For the first time since she'd met him, he wasn't wearing it. His hair was trimmed around his ears, but long on top. It shone with auburn highlights. And now that his eyes weren't shadowed by the bill of his cap, Jas could see that they were fringed with enviably long lashes.

"So what else did you and Danvers talk about?" he asked, sitting next to her on the sofa.

"What do you mean, 'what else'?" she asked, scooting away from him.

"I *mean,* what was that stuff about Whirlwind?"

Jas was surprised by his question. "How do you know about Whirlwind?"

"You think I don't know why you're here? I may be goofy-looking, but I'm not stupid."

"You're not goofy-looking," Jas argued, flushing when she realized what she'd said. "I mean— oh, forget it," she snapped.

He grinned. "I knew you liked me."

"I do not." Jas slumped back into the sofa cushions. "So how do you know about me and Whirlwind? *Miss Hahn?*" she spat.

"No. My dad's an investigator with the Stanford Police Department."

"What?" Jas shot upright. "And he's been telling you all about me!"

Chase shrugged. "Hey, it's not like that stuff is confidential. A kid breaks the law and anybody can find out about it."

"Yes, but, but..." Jas sputtered, "but why were you asking him about *me*?" she accused. Then she frowned. "Oh, I get it. You wanted to find out all the dirt on the juvenile delinquent staying with *Diane*."

"That's not why," Chase said, his ears turning pink.

"Need help setting the table!" Miss Hahn hollered from the kitchen. "The chicken's almost done!"

"I'll help." Chase stood up so fast that Jas bounced on the sofa cushion. "I hope you have enough food," he called as he bolted for the kitchen. "Dr. Danvers is coming to dinner."

"Dr. Danvers!" She stuck her head around the door frame, place mats in her hand.

"I invited him when I heard he was having a frozen dinner," Jas explained hastily. "I know I should have asked you first, but I could hear him drooling when I mentioned fried chicken."

Miss Hahn looped a strand of hair over one ear. "No. No. That was a good idea. Gosh, should I change?"

"No, you look great," Chase said.

"Except I'm so dirty." Miss Hahn plucked at her pant leg, then began fanning herself with the place mats. "Whoo-wee, is it hot in here or is it just me?"

Jas looked over at Chase, who wiggled his brows at her and mouthed, "I told you."

Jas burst out laughing, feeling some of the tension go away.

"You two are acting mighty strange," Miss Hahn declared. Handing Chase the place mats, she hurried through the living room and up the steps, saying, "I'm changing into something else. Set the table for me, Chase."

He saluted. "Aye-aye, Captain."

When he went into the kitchen, Jas sat for a minute. *So Chase's dad is an investigator. Maybe he would be able to help me.*

But that would have to wait for later. She still didn't have enough proof to go to the police. She had figured out *how* Hugh had arranged Whirlwind's death. But now she needed to find out *why.* Jas figured that Hugh's insurance policy might give her the "why." If the mare was healthy, she would have been more valuable alive than dead. *Unless* Hugh had a huge insurance policy on her.

Jas knew where Hugh kept the files on the

horses. And Phil had access to them at any time. But would he help?

After listening to make sure everybody was busy, Jas picked up the phone and dialed the office number for High Meadows. Phil just might be there taking care of last-minute paperwork before leaving for the night.

He picked up on the first ring.

"Phil, it's Jas." Furtively, she glanced up the steps, checking to see if Miss Hahn was coming down. This was one conversation she definitely didn't want her to report to Hugh.

"Jas?" Phil's voice was just as low. Was someone in the office with him?

"I heard you went to see Grandfather," Jas rushed on. "I heard you suspect Hugh of putting the yew in the paddock."

There was a dead silence. Jas bit her bottom lip.

"Yes."

"Then you've got to help me! I need to look at Whirlwind's insurance policy. I think it's the key to proving Hugh killed her. Can you get me a copy?"

"Yes. Look, I've got to go. I'll meet you at one o'clock Wednesday when you visit the nursing home. I'll have it then."

The phone clicked off. For a second, Jas didn't

move, afraid she'd burst the bubble of hope swelling inside her. If everything worked out, she finally had an idea how to get Hugh.

A copy of Dr. Danvers's autopsy report stating that Whirlwind's stomach was empty would show how Hugh planned to kill Whirlwind. A copy of the insurance policy showing a big payoff would then show his motivation to do so.

The police might not believe her, but how could they ignore the documents? And with Phil on her side, she would finally be able to prove that Hugh Robicheaux killed his own horse.

Chapter 14

"I'll pick you up in half an hour," Miss Hahn said as Jas climbed out of the car. It was Wednesday, the day of Jas's second visit with her grandfather.

Miss Hahn pulled out of the driveway to go run some errands. As Jas walked up the sidewalk, she began to feel nervous.

Is Phil really coming?

But as soon as she scanned the cars, she spotted Phil's Jeep parked behind the nursing home van. Excited, she rushed inside, checked in at the front desk, and then hunted for Phil and her grandfather. She found both of them in the dayroom. Phil was standing by the window wearing new jeans and cowboy boots, looking totally ill at ease.

"Hi!" Jas rushed over to her grandfather's wheelchair. Crouching by his knee, she took his hand and peered into his pale face. He smiled crookedly, but his eyes seemed brighter.

"Did Phil tell you what he was bringing us?"

Grandfather nodded, but when she glanced up at Phil, she saw distress etched in his face. "What's wrong?" Jas asked as she stood up. "Couldn't you get a copy of the policy?"

"I got one," Phil said as he twisted his John Deere hat in his hands. "Only it's not going to prove nothing." Pulling several papers from his back pocket, he thrust them at her.

Jas's mouth went dry. Slowly, she unfolded the papers. Phil pointed to several lines at the bottom of the first sheet. "Whirlwind was only insured for fifty grand," he said. "But she was worth a hundred."

"But that can't be!" Jas cried in disbelief. "If Hugh lost money on the mare, he would have had no reason to kill her!"

Phil bobbed his head. "That's right." He glanced at Grandfather, who was staring so intently at both of them that Jas could tell he was taking in every word.

"Which means we've got to drop this whole thing," Phil said as he lowered his voice. "Hugh knows we're suspicious."

A chill raced up Jas's spine. "How does he know? *What* does he know?"

Phil swung his head. "I'm not sure. But he knows I visited your grandfather last Saturday.

And I think he knows I'm here with you today."

Jas let out her breath. "I bet Miss Hahn told him. Do you think he knows about this copy?"

"Probably. The guy's been watching me like a hawk. He's looking for any excuse to fire me. You know that Danvers isn't our vet anymore?"

"Ummph!" Jas glanced down at Grandfather, who sounded as if he was being strangled. Kneeling, she patted his hand. "Are you all right?"

"At ooves Hugh illed Irlwind!" He waved his good arm wildly.

"Are you saying that getting rid of Danvers proves Hugh is guilty?" Jas clarified.

"Es! Ee's etting id of all of us."

Jas's eyes widened. "He's right. Hugh is getting rid of anyone who might be suspicious about Whirlwind's death. That shows he is guilty of *something*, but what?"

"Danvers had his doubts about the mare's death," said Phil. "So when he did the autopsy, he checked to make sure she was sound. He also made sure she was still valuable as a brood mare. She was. That means if Hugh killed her, he killed a perfectly healthy mare worth over a hundred thousand dollars. Which makes *no* sense."

Jas stifled a moan. How could she have been so wrong? Was there something she was missing?

Aladdin!

"Phil, tell me about Aladdin."

"Aladdin?" Phil frowned in confusion.

"That horse that died the year my grand-parents and I came to work at the farm. He was that big Dutch Warmblood. He used to jump into the field to chase the cattle. Hugh always boasted he could jump over the moon."

"I remember him," Phil said. "A chestnut gelding. Died of colic."

"Did anyone check to make sure it really was colic?"

"Danvers was called in—he was the vet back then, too—and he said all the signs pointed to colic."

"What about an autopsy?"

"Wasn't done. Aladdin was only insured for thirty thousand. Usually, the horse has to be insured for fifty thousand or more for the insurance company to do a full-scale investigation. Besides, his death wasn't suspicious."

Jas tapped her lip, another thought crossing her mind. "What if Dr. Danvers is in on the scam with Hugh?" she said to Phil. "What if he faked Whirlwind's autopsy report?"

"Oh!" Grandfather protested.

"Your grandfather's right," Phil said. "I'd trust Danvers with *my* life. Besides, he's the one who did the extra tests on Whirlwind because he was suspicious."

He patted Jas's shoulder with his work-roughened hand. "When I checked the insurance policy, I called Danvers. He mentioned that you two had talked about Whirlwind's stomach being empty. That's not enough evidence against Hugh." Ducking his head, he looked down at his hat as if ashamed. "The two of us agreed to drop the whole thing." Phil paused and then grabbed Jas's shoulder. "You need to also, Jas."

Her heart sank because it seemed Phil was right. The insurance policy only proved Hugh would have been crazy to kill his own horse.

"Maybe it *was* an accident that the yew got in Whirlwind's paddock," said Phil as he put on his cap. "I'm sorry, guys, but I've got to go. Hugh thinks I'm at the hardware store."

"Thanks for coming," said Jas dully.

A small smile creased Phil's leathery face. "Forget about the past, Jas. Your grandfather is mending fast. When he gets out of here, some horse farm will be eager to hire him. Everybody knows your grandfather is the greatest."

"I guess." Tears filled her eyes. She hoped Grandfather didn't realize what Phil *wasn't* saying.

Her grandfather *was* the greatest. He'd never

be able to pull his own weight again. If no one would hire a partially crippled man as a caretaker, what would happen to them?

As if he knew what she was thinking, Grandfather reached up, took her hand, and held on tightly to his granddaughter.

Shadow's rough orange hair was falling out in clumps. Jas ran the curry comb against the grain of his coat. Underneath, the new hair was a shiny chestnut color.

She wrapped her arms around the big horse's neck. "You're going to be beautiful! Soon that white exclamation point on your face will stand for WOW!"

He turned to look at her, a hunk of hay hanging from his mouth. Since Shadow was out of quarantine, he'd been moved to the big barn.

"Okay, maybe not beautiful," she teased. "You're too big and gawky. But if you keep eating like a pig, you'll soon be as fat as Lassie."

It was the end of June, fifteen days since Jas had been at Second Chance Farm. Eight days since Shadow had been on the thyroid treatment. Already he looked better. His back was still bony and his hind legs stiff, but Jas could tell by the gleam in his eyes and the arch of his neck that he was feeling like a new horse.

Sighing, she rested against his shoulder. Thank goodness she'd been busy the past week. In addition to yard work and taking care of Shadow, the farm had hosted a dozen kids' groups over the weekend. So she didn't have that much time to dwell on the meeting. But whenever she did have a moment's rest, like right now, the disappointment made Jas frustrated. How can I prove Hugh is guilty when there is no evidence?

Suddenly someone shouted and completely interrupted Jas's thoughts. Curious, she walked over to the stall's back window and looked outside.

Lucy was riding a fat pinto in one of the paddocks. Although she wasn't a horrible rider, she did flap and flop around like a duckling learning to fly.

"Lucy, relax and go *with* the horse's movement," Miss Hahn was saying patiently. Miss Hahn was leaning on the paddock fence with her back to Jas. Chase was standing next to Miss Hahn.

"I'm trying, but this horse has a killer trot!"

"If she was bouncing like that on my back, I'd try to throw her off, too," Chase said to Miss Hahn from behind his hand.

Jas stifled a laugh. Patting Shadow, she went

into the aisle and closed his stall door. She dropped the currycomb in the grooming box, then walked outside to join them.

"What's Lucy doing?" Jas asked as she came up beside Miss Hahn.

"You had trouble figuring that out, too?" Chase joked.

Miss Hahn blew out a breath of frustration. "We're trying to get Spots ready to adopt. He's pretty hardheaded, and I don't want someone taking him home and immediately getting bucked off."

"Where did he come from?" Jas asked.

"He was living in the woods like some wild animal," Chase said. "When he started raiding cornfields, the farmers complained to the police. We had to rope him to catch him."

"That's it!" Lucy yelled in complete frustration. Halting Spots in front of them, she jumped off. "I'm never riding this horse again."

Jerking the reins over the horse's head, Lucy thrust them at Miss Hahn. "For all I care, he can be sold for dog food!"

Hands on her slim hips, she glared at them as if waiting for a rebuke. Ducking his head, Chase laughed behind his palm. Jas started to giggle.

"What are you two laughing about?" Lucy snapped. "I bet greenhorn couldn't do any better."

She jabbed her thumb in Jas's direction.

Jas swallowed her laughter. "Oh, really?" said Jas.

Taking the reins from Miss Hahn, Jas climbed over the fence and jumped to the ground so close to Lucy that the other girl stumbled backward.

"May I borrow your helmet?" Jas asked politely.

"Sure." Lucy didn't sound quite so cocky as Jas confidently pulled the helmet on. Even Chase had stopped laughing.

Without a word, Jas led Spots around the paddock while massaging the crest of his neck. She had retrained several "hardheaded" horses, and she knew that most of them were hardheaded because their riders used kicks and jerks to force them to obey commands. But it *had* been over a month since she'd been on a horse. Would she remember what to do?

As Jas turned Spots in small circles, the horse watched her suspiciously with one blue eye. Ignoring his nasty look, she continued to massage his neck. When he finally heaved a sigh, and she could no longer see the whites of his eyes, Jas mounted him. Instantly, Spots stiffened.

"I won't ask you to do anything you aren't ready for," she assured him as she rubbed his withers.

"What *is* she doing?" she heard Lucy hiss impatiently.

Jas tuned her out. In fact, she tuned out everything except Spots. Riding wasn't just about sitting on a horse. It was about communication.

They stood there for ten minutes until she felt Spots relax. Only then did she pick up the reins and nudge his sides gently with her heels.

He walked hollow-backed, with his nose in the air, as if preparing for something horrible to happen. But Jas held the reins lightly and steered him around the paddock, using only weight shifts and leg pressure instead of tugs and kicks. After what seemed like forever, Spots dropped his nose, flexed his neck, and rounded his back.

"Big deal. So she can make the horse walk," Lucy grumbled loudly.

Only, Jas didn't care what Lucy thought. She could feel Spots's stride growing looser and longer. She could feel her body flowing with the rhythm of his gait as her muscles instinctively remembered what to do.

As they walked around the paddock, the thudding of Spots's hooves on the ground sent waves of joy through Jas. Tears welled in her eyes, and she realized how much she'd missed riding all these weeks.

But then, suddenly, came the same gut-wrenching feeling of loss she felt when Whirlwind had died. She knew she belonged on a horse. But when Grandfather got out of the nursing home, they would have to move into an apartment.

Once Jas left Second Chance Farm, there would be no room or time for horses. She would probably never ride again.

Chapter 15

"Ouch," Jas squealed. This time Shadow had gotten her, his big teeth pinching her skin along with her T-shirt. Swinging his head around, Shadow pricked his ears, as if to say, "Look how cute I am!" Jas frowned and pointed the brush at him.

"You are *not* cute," she scolded. "In fact, you're due for a reality check. You may be bigger and stronger, but you keep forgetting that I'm the dominant one in this herd."

He bobbed his head, as if to agree with her. But Jas could tell by his devilish expression that he didn't believe a word she said. As if to prove it, he kicked out with his front hoof, striking the wall of the stall.

Jas rolled her eyes. It was the Fourth of July weekend, over two weeks since they'd brought Shadow to the farm. He was still lean, but he'd gotten so sassy that Jas had already cut out his special feed and turned him out all night in a bigger paddock. But that wasn't doing the trick. Shadow had turned into a high-spirited brat.

Since she had to groom him in the stall, she had to be extra careful. When she'd first seen him at the auction, she guessed his height at about sixteen-three hands. Now his head didn't hang and his body didn't sag, and she figured he was closer to seventeen hands, with legs like tree trunks and a girth like a barrel. For her own safety, she couldn't let him buffalo her.

Taking up a little slack on the lead, she continued to brush him. Only this time, she watched him out of the corner of her eye. When she hit a ticklish spot and he swung his big teeth around, she raised her elbow and popped him hard in the muzzle.

Startled, Shadow jerked his head up and stared at Jas in surprise. She just went about what she was doing and ignored him. When he raised his front hoof to strike, she growled "no" and whapped him on the shoulder with the end of the lead.

Indignant and hurt, he gave her a puzzled look. Then he lowered his head and nudged her with his nose. Laughing, she scratched his forehead.

"I forgive you. Just remember: I'm the lead horse in this herd. Once you know this, we'll get along great." She let out her breath, knowing that she'd have to be on her toes every minute. She also knew what a horse like Shadow really needed—riding, at least two hours a day.

For the past three days, Jas had been working Spots and a quiet mare named Flower. And she'd had a blast. But even though Jas had been riding since she was four, she'd never met a horse like Shadow. She was used to fine-boned hunters, bred for grace and confirmation. Shadow was like an out-of-control freight train.

A loud banging from the feed room told Jas that Chase had arrived for the evening feeding. She dropped her brush in the grooming box and unhooked Shadow's lead.

As she shut the door behind her, Chase came up the aisle with feed buckets swinging from each hand. "Can I help you feed?" she asked him.

"Why would you want to do that?" Chase responded. Without looking at her, he dropped the buckets in front of the last stall and started scooping out grain. Excited nickers rang up and down the aisle.

"Why would the famous equestrienne lower herself to doing humble chores?"

"Knock it off, Chase," Jas fumed. "You're being a jerk. I just want to help."

This time he looked up. "*I'm* being a jerk?" He

poked his thumb into his chest. "Have *I* been the one swaggering around the barn since *I* rode Spots last Tuesday? Have *I* been the one with my nose stuck in the air as *I* talk about doing dressage with this horse and eventing with that horse? Nooooo," he answered his own question. "I've been mucking stalls, mending fences, cleaning wounds, sweeping…"

Jas raised one hand. "All right. You made your point. I haven't been pulling my weight. I was just so excited about riding again that I got carried away."

"You *and* Miss Hahn," he grumbled. "It's like she's forgotten the purpose of the farm." Pushing past Jas, he dumped feed through a slot into one of the tubs. "She thinks she's back on her father's fancy-shmancy horse farm. You know, she used to be a horse snob, just like you."

"I'm *not* a horse snob!" Jas protested, following after him as he went down to the next stall. "And what's wrong with being excited about riding?"

"We're suppose to be *rescuing* animals."

Jas propped her fists on her hips. "You know what, Chase? I think you're the one who's a snob. You like horses only when they're abused or sick."

"Not true. I just don't think they have to win

some ribbon to be worth something." He scowled at her as he went over to Shadow's stall.

"Who's said anything about winning ribbons?" Jas snapped. "We're talking about riding. Look how much better Spots is since I've been riding him. He's not perfect, but he's not such a hardheaded sourpuss, either, like you."

"Spare me the insults," Chase snorted. Striding past her, he continued down the aisle, the stiff set of his shoulders telling Jas that she was getting nowhere.

Oh, why do I even bother with him? she fumed at herself. *Communicating with Spots is a lot easier.*

She looked into Shadow's stall. He was attacking the feed in his tub as if it was his last meal. She'd wait until he finished eating, then turn him out for the night.

"You want to know why I'm really mad?" Chase suddenly asked right behind her. When Jas turned to look at him, the hurt in his eyes took her by surprise.

"Why?" she asked as her stomach tightened.

"Because...because...because I can't ride worth a damn."

A giggle of relief bubbled in Jas's throat.

"I knew you'd think it was dumb." He whipped around to leave, but Jas caught his wrist.

"Wait."

Chase stopped, although he refused to look at her. Jas kept her hand on his arm, his skin warm under her touch. Slowly, she slid her fingers down his wrist until they met his palm. Almost desperately, he laced his fingers with hers.

"What's wrong with not being able to ride?" she asked, her heart thumping.

He slanted his face toward her. "Nothing. At least I never thought anything about it until I saw you ride. I mean, when I watch Lucy ride, I want to sympathize with the horse. When I watch you ride a horse, it's…it's…" He rubbed his forehead in frustration. "Dang, I really stink at explaining stuff like this."

Jas waited.

"It's like watching two people dance," he said quickly. "How's that for dopey?"

Jas smiled shyly at him. "I thought it was nice."

"Well, you would." He dragged the toe of his tennis shoe in the dirt.

"So you want me to teach you how to ride?"

"No. At least not now. I'd be too embarrassed. Maybe later when…" His voice trailed off, and his eyes flicked toward her.

Jas's heart skipped a beat. *Maybe later when we know each other better? Was that what you were about to say?*

"Anyway, I really like taking care of the horses," he rushed on. "Doctoring them, that kind of stuff. For now, I'll let you do the riding."

He grinned crookedly, and Jas suddenly realized how close they were standing to each other. So close, in fact, that all she had to do was tip her head up and he could kiss her. At the thought of his lips touching hers, Jas's cheeks flamed and she stepped backward. Her fingers slipped from his grasp. "So can I help you feed?"

"Sure." He reached for a bucket, his neck as red as her cheeks.

Jas picked up Shadow's lead line. "Let me just turn out the brat," she said. "He's finished eating."

"Put him out with Jinx," Chase suggested.

Shadow was licking the bottom of his feed tub, trying to get every last kernel. When she hooked the lead to his halter ring, he lunged for the open door.

"Whoa," she barked, digging in her heels so he wouldn't pull her with him. He stopped in his tracks. "Good boy." She scratched his shoulder, then made him move when she wanted.

Obediently, he walked down the aisle until he saw Jinx, then he arched his neck and pranced sideways. Jas told him to walk, and when he ignored her, she reminded him with a swift snap of the lead.

Jinx was in the middle of the field, grazing. Shadow danced in place, eager to join him. Jas led him through the gate and then shut it. She then made him stand for a second.

When she unhooked the lead and stepped away, Shadow exploded–bucking and rearing across the pasture. Jinx raised his head and gazed with disinterest.

"Man, is he something," Chase said, coming up beside her. "I never thought the dull-eyed horse we bought at that auction would ever end up like that."

"I had no idea, either," Jas admitted as she watched Shadow trot across the pasture, snapping his legs like a dressage horse doing a Grand Prix movement. "I wish I knew the story behind him."

"Really, even I can tell he was once somebody's *valuable* blue-ribbon winner." Chase shot her a teasing look.

"Oh, shut up," Jas said as she punched him on the arm. For a second, they stood side by side, their hips touching, watching Shadow show off. Jas rested her arms on the top board. For the first time in what seemed like forever, she felt happy.

Shadow nipped at Jinx's flank. When he didn't get any reaction, he cantered to the far end of the paddock and stared into the next field, where the neighbor's cattle grazed. Raising his head high, he whinnied loudly at them. Then without warning, he galloped toward the fence and jumped over it as if it wasn't even there.

Jas and Chase gaped in astonishment.

"Did you see that?" Chase exclaimed. "That fence is at least five feet, and Shadow practically stepped over it!"

Jas shook her head in disbelief. "I've never seen a horse jump like that."

On the other side of the fence, Shadow galloped around the cattle, who scattered like startled deer.

Jas's heart skipped a beat. Suddenly, she realized who Shadow reminded her of—Aladdin—the horse that could jump over the moon.

No, that's crazy. Hugh's horse has been dead five years. This has got to be just a coincidence.

"Old Man Hopkins is going to be furious if he sees one of our horses chasing his cows," Chase said. "He's always looking for an excuse to close us down. We better go catch Shadow." Putting one hand on the top board, he vaulted over the fence.

"I'll get a bucket of grain." Jas dashed into the barn, grabbed the feed bucket, and ran after Chase, who had climbed into the neighbor's pasture. With a toss of his head, Shadow pranced around Chase as if they were playing a game of tag. Jas was scaling the fence with the bucket in her hand when Shadow suddenly swerved and thundered right at her. Quickly, she flattened her body against the top board. It looked as if Shadow was going to run right into the fence—and Jas. But at the last second he effortlessly leaped over the fence and back into his paddock.

Jas's jaw dropped. Shadow cleared her by a foot!

Shadow slid to a halt, and with a pleased look, trotted over to Jas and stuck his head in the feed bucket, almost ripping it from her hand. Taking a huge bite, he lifted his head, tossing grain right and left. Beside him, Jinx greedily picked kernels off the ground.

"Wow!" Chase jogged up, sweat rolling down his cheeks. "I'm going to have to add another board to that fence!"

"Make that two boards," Jas gasped.

Chase shook his head in disbelief. "What are we going to do with him? He can't just go jumping in and out whenever he wants."

"One thing we're *not* going to do is tell Miss Hahn."

"Why not?"

"Because if Hopkins complains, she might get rid of him," Jas said quickly.

Chase gave her a skeptical look. "Diane wouldn't do that. What's the *real* reason, Jas?"

"I can't tell you," she said, hoping that he'd understand. Not that she totally understood herself. But if there was some strange chance Shadow was connected to Hugh, she didn't want Miss Hahn reporting it.

"You know, Jas, you've got a lot of secrets to keep to yourself," Chase said. "One day you're going to have to trust somebody."

"I know." Reaching down, she ruffled Shadow's forelock. She couldn't look at Chase. "I'm just not quite ready yet."

"So what are we going to do with the big gorilla?" said Chase as he climbed the fence and sat beside Jas, with his heels propped on the center board.

Jas tapped her lip, wondering the same thing. Maybe Shadow wasn't Aladdin, but he was definitely the most powerful jumper she'd ever seen. And if his little show was any indication, he obviously thought leaping over obstacles was child's play.

The trouble was finding a rider who could handle him. Jas eyed the big horse as he happily sprayed grain everywhere. Slowly, she grinned.

"I know exactly what we're going to do with Shadow," Jas said as she leaped off the top board into the paddock. "We're going to turn him into the best jumper in the state."

"Oh, really?" Chase sounded unconvinced. "And who's going to ride him?"

Standing on her tiptoes, Jas threw her arm over Shadow's withers, her grin spreading wider.

"I am!"

Chapter 16

Aladdin.

The death of that horse five years ago was driving Jas crazy. Even though she knew there was no way Shadow could be Aladdin, the similarities were too eerie.

It was Tuesday morning, and Jas was sitting at the kitchen table with Ms. Tomlinson. Before she had tuned the social worker out, they'd been discussing her monthly allowance. Usually, Jas was interested in money. But this afternoon, she could have cared less.

What was really bugging her was the way Hugh had thrown out Aladdin's name when he called her that first day. As if he was deliberately taunting her. Even if Aladdin had nothing to do with Shadow, Jas was convinced the horse had something to do with Whirlwind's death. It seemed Hugh thought that Jas wasn't smart enough to figure out the connection. This time, Jas was going to prove him wrong.

She had seen Aladdin only once or twice before he died. Phil had said he was big and chestnut-colored. Jas racked her brain, trying to remember more about the horse. But it had been so long ago, and she'd been very young.

Phil must have a photo, thought Jas.

Tomorrow afternoon, Jas was visiting Grandfather. If she could just get Phil to bring a picture of Aladdin to the nursing home, she would be able to tell if Shadow and Aladdin were the same horse. And if they weren't, then she would focus on finding the link between Aladdin's and Whirlwind's deaths.

Miss Hahn had a school group coming to the farm during Jas's lockdown time this afternoon. That would be the perfect time to call Phil at High Meadows.

"Any questions, Jas?" Ms. Tomlinson's voice broke into her thoughts.

"Uh, no." She had no idea what Ms. Tomlinson had been saying.

"Miss Hahn said you need new tennis shoes," the social worker went on. "I know how expensive those brand names can be. So remember, the money is for the whole month. If you spend it all at once…"

Forget new sneakers, Jas thought. The black-smith was coming this afternoon, and she was going to spend her money on horseshoes for Shadow. She'd lunged him several times since his big adventure in the cattle field. He'd surprised her by walking, trotting, and cantering like a gentleman. Now he was ready to ride.

"...and you can save the rest for toiletries."

"Don't worry," Jas assured her glibly. "I'll get sneakers at Payless and have plenty of money left over."

"Payless is a wise choice." Ms. Tomlinson blinked her watery eyes, then sneezed. Jas tipped the chair in an attempt to get away from the germs.

"I have one more matter to discuss." Dabbing her nose, the social worker opened the file folder and rummaged through the stack of papers. "I contacted your mother."

"What!" Jas dropped the chair back to the floor.

"I've contacted your mother. She's living in Florida."

"You mean my *birth* mother," Jas corrected hotly. "That woman in Florida doesn't qualify as a mother. She never took care of me."

"I realize that," Ms. Tomlinson said. "But she is a relative, and we had to contact her. I was finally able to reach her yesterday."

Jas looked out the screen door, wanting to

focus on anything but what Ms. Tomlinson was going to say. Lassie and Reese were staring into the kitchen. When they realized that someone had noticed them, they wagged their tails excitedly.

"Your 'birth' mother said that her circumstances are such that she is unable to be your guardian at this time," Ms. Tomlinson continued, her tone matter-of-fact.

Just say she doesn't want me, Jas thought bitterly. *I've heard it plenty of times before.*

"That means you'll remain in the custody of social services until your grandfather is better. I'm sorry, Jas."

Jas snorted. "Don't be. My grandparents raised me. *They* were my mother and father."

"And your grandfather *is* getting better." Ms. Tomlinson smiled, happy to give her some good news.

"Yes," Jas replied, trying to sound pleased. But she could feel herself hardening inside. *Why did she have to bring up my mother?*

Iris Schuler had abandoned Jas when she was two. "It's not that she doesn't love you," her grandparents had patiently explained.

Jas knew the whole story—at least the one her grandparents told. Iris had been only sixteen when she'd gotten pregnant, and like Jas, she'd lived and breathed horses.

As soon as Jas was born, Iris had quit high school to work at the racetrack. For the next two years, she jockeyed, which was a life unfit for a mother. So she'd given up all rights, and Jas's grandparents eagerly adopted her. After that, Iris moved to Florida, and except for letters and Christmas cards, Jas had lost track of her.

Not that she'd cared. With her grandparents' love, she'd pushed her mother out of her mind, even though it wasn't always easy.

"Any questions before I leave? Any problems with the ankle bracelet?" Ms. Tomlinson asked. "You've been on probation now for four weeks, and Mrs. Weisgerber reports that everything's been fine."

"No problems. When is my next hearing?"

"Probably the middle of August."

Jas shot to her feet. "But that'll be more than forty-five days!" she protested. "I'm supposed to be back in court the beginning of August."

Ms. Tomlinson nodded. "I know." She patted the seat of Jas's chair. "Sit down and let me explain."

Jas sat slowly with a stiff spine.

"There's a reason for delaying the hearing. I've talked to Dr. Bindera. She thinks your grandfather can be released at the beginning of August.

Social Services needs to get him settled in an apartment so we can recommend that you be placed with him."

"Oh," Jas said sheepishly. "That's actually great news."

"But, Jas, I need to warn you." Ms. Tomlinson wadded up a tissue and looked uncomfortable. "If your grandfather's in no condition to take care of you, then you may have to stay in foster care."

Jas whipped one hand up like a stop sign. "I don't want to hear it. He's going to be okay."

Ms. Tomlinson dipped her head. "Just so you understand." Standing, she closed her briefcase. "I'm going to report in to Miss Hahn, so I'll see you in several weeks."

Once Ms. Tomlinson was gone, Jas made a fist and pounded the table. Of course Grandfather was going to be fine. He *had* to be fine. She loved him too much, and there was no way she was going to stay in foster care forever.

Especially since her mother didn't want her. Anger rushed through Jas's veins. If Ms. Tomlinson had contacted Iris in Florida, then she must know that her father was sick and in a nursing home. She must know that her daughter had been convicted of a crime and was in foster care.

How could she not care?

Hugging her arms around her chest, Jas struggled against the rage that threatened to engulf her. Her mother had disappointed her so many times that by now Jas knew what to do.

She had to think about how much her grandmother had loved her and how much her grandfather did love her.

Forget her. Forget her, Jas silently chanted. Concentrate on Grandfather and Shadow...and getting out of foster care as soon as possible.

"This horse has big strong hooves with a good wall," Pete the blacksmith announced from underneath Shadow's belly. He had the horse's left front leg anchored between his thighs as he filed the hoof's rough edges.

"Do you think just front shoes will be okay?" Jas asked. "I can't afford all four."

"Sure." Dropping the foot, the blacksmith straightened and rubbed the small of his back. "Glad he's the last today."

When Pete went out to his truck, Jas stroked Shadow's neck. He stood quietly, chewing the end of the lead line when he got restless, pinning his ears back when the blacksmith walked in front of him.

"You're such a faker," Jas teased.

"Lucky I got his size," Pete said, holding up two shoes when he came back in.

"You don't have many horses with hooves his size?" she asked.

"Nope, not at all."

Jas shifted from foot to foot, wanting to ask Pete a dozen questions. According to Chase, Pete had been shoeing forever. There was always a chance he might know something about Shadow or Aladdin.

"Do you know Hugh Robicheaux?" Jas asked.

"Nope."

"Have you ever seen a horse like Shadow around the area?" Pete had clients up and down the Shenandoah Valley.

"Nope. Would have remembered a horse this big who wasn't a draft breed. Where'd Miss Hahn get him?"

"The auction at Mountain Royal. A guy named Reaves sold him."

Pete humphed. "Reaves, huh. That guy would cheat his mother. Word has it that a lot of the horses he buys and sells are hot."

"You mean stolen?"

"Yeah. He has a place in the hills in Page County. Turns out that he keeps the horses he buys in a field until he has a truckload of them. Then he takes them to the auction for quick money," said Pete.

"Looking at these old nail holes, this horse had shoes on all four feet not too long ago," he continued.

"How long ago?"

"About eight or nine weeks, which means Reaves didn't have him long. He doesn't spend money on feed, much less shoes."

Jas remembered what Danvers had said about Shadow's condition. Judging from the horse's grown-out rough coat and the weight loss, Danvers had guessed that he'd been sick for at least three months. That meant he'd been sick when Reaves bought him.

Jas knew that a thyroid condition in horses was unusual. So when Shadow couldn't perform anymore and his owners had no idea why, and the vet bills began to pour in, his owners must have dumped him.

"Poor guy," Jas crooned, kissing him on his velvety muzzle. But truthfully, she was glad he'd been dumped, because there was no way his former owners could have loved him as much as she did.

Reaching under his forelock, she scratched an itchy spot. He wiggled his lips with delight. Jas laughed at his silly expression. But then her smile quickly faded. Although she'd been pre-

tending that Shadow was her horse, she knew he wasn't. He was Miss Hahn's. Although Jas didn't trust her, she knew that if it hadn't been for Miss Hahn and her crazy farm, Shadow would never have had his second chance.

Chapter 17

"Grandfather!" Jas's mouth fell open in surprise. Using a walker for support, Grandfather met Jas at the front door of the nursing home.

He grinned like a little kid. "Ow do you like my new wheels?" he crowed.

"I love them! How long have you been walking?"

"Two ays. To surprise oo."

Jas kissed his soft, saggy cheek. "You surprised me all right."

Dressed in his jeans, suspenders, and denim shirt, he *almost* looked like his old self. Not that either of them would ever be the same again.

Moving the walker in a circle, he slowly started back toward his room. He made his way down the hall, first setting the walker in front of him, then sliding his feet forward.

"Is Phil here?" Jas asked.

"No," he puffed. He was stooped over the

walker, his arms trembling. The short trip had exhausted him.

When they were almost to his room, Jas ran ahead and pushed his wheelchair to the doorway. "Here. You look like you've had enough."

She maneuvered it behind him. With a groan, he sank into the seat. "Thank oo."

"Whew. That was quite an adventure!" Jas wiped her brow, feeling almost as worn out as he did. "I'm so proud of you. You've made such terrific progress," she said as he pushed his chair into his room, which was sparsely furnished with two twin beds, a small dresser, and a plastic-covered chair.

"I...have...made...good...progress." Jas's grandfather pronounced each word slowly but perfectly. Jas grinned, and when he grinned back, both sides of his mouth tipped up.

"There you guys are," said Phil as he hurried into the room with a long box under his arm. Jas's heart skipped a beat. *Did he bring a photo of Aladdin?*

"I have a present for you. From *Hugh*." He set the box on Grandfather's lap. "I can't stay," he rushed on. "Hugh and I are headed to Kentucky for two days."

"What about the picture of Aladdin?" Jas asked. Phil's face grew tight. "I didn't bring one.

Jas...um. Look, I think you need to drop this obsession of yours."

"Obsession! You call finding Whirlwind's killer an obsess...?"

"Jas!" Grandfather's sharp voice cut her off. "Enough."

Openmouthed, Jas stared at him. Had he given up, too?

"He's right, Jas," Phil agreed. "The issue is dead."

Jas narrowed her eyes. "You sound like you're on Hugh's side," she accused, noticing that for the first time since she could remember, Phil wasn't carrying his John Deere cap. Instead, he was clutching a tweed sport cap similar to the one Hugh wore.

Phil shook his head wearily. "No, I'm not. I'm just trying to be realistic. Whirlwind is dead. Nothing will bring her back. Besides, I have no idea what Aladdin has to do with her death." Hastily, he patted Grandfather's shoulder. "Karl, I'll visit when we get back. Good-bye, Jas."

She didn't reply, and when he left, her spirits tumbled. She couldn't believe Phil had turned traitor. Who would help her now?

Grandfather held up the box. "Let's ook at the present."

Jas helped him open it. Inside was a polished silver-handled cane.

"Andsome," Grandfather said as he tapped the rubber-tipped end on the floor.

"It's just a payoff from Hugh the murderer," Jas groused.

Grandfather winked at her. "Don't worry, oo'll get your ph-photo."

"How?"

"Hugh's album."

"That's right. You helped him keep his photo album up-to-date. Where is it?"

"The office in the arn."

"Oh, great." Dejected, Jas plopped down on his bed. "I'm not supposed to set foot on the farm."

"Hugh and Phil will be gone for oo days." Smiling slyly, he bumped her on the leg with the cane. "You'll f-figure out a way. Ust don't get caught!"

Jas burst out laughing. "You really are a sly old fox, aren't you?"

He wiggled his shaggy brows. "I want to get Hugh as much as oo do!"

"Ten dollars for your thoughts?" Chase asked later that night. He and Jas were sitting on the porch swing playing cards. A warm breeze ruffled Jas's hair, and the moon shone down brightly in the night sky. Crickets and frogs chirped in the trees, and Angel and Lassie snored on the steps.

"I thought it was a penny for your thoughts," Jas said.

Chase shrugged. "Well, I thought with inflation and all," he said as he laid down his cards between them. "Gin."

"Gin?" Confused, Jas stared at her own cards. She'd arranged them in a poker hand, totally forgetting what game they were playing. Her mind had been so focused on the photo album and the impossible task of retrieving it that she was playing the wrong game.

With a sigh, she turned her cards facedown. "Sorry. I haven't been paying much attention."

"I'll say. I wish we'd been playing for money. I would have big money."

"Only I don't have big money. My fortune went for Shadow's horseshoes."

"Then I guess we'll have to play for something else." He arched one brow and grinned.

"Like what?" Tilting her head, Jas eyed him.

His hair was smooth and shiny as if he'd blown it dry, and he wore jean shorts and sandals. His legs were pale and covered with downy blond hair that looked so soft that Jas wanted to skim her fingers over it.

He pushed off with both feet, and the swing began to rock. "Every time I win, I get to ask you a question. That way, I can find out what's going on in your head. You've been as tight as a girth on a fat pony."

"Oh." Jas looked away. Since the big blowup over Fourth of July weekend, being with Chase had become much easier. It was even fun. Every morning and night, she helped him feed and doctor the horses. But she still didn't want to answer his questions or tell him what was bugging her. Since Whirlwind's death, her trusting side was like a sealed envelope.

Chase picked up the cards and shuffled them expertly. "So what do you think?"

"Does that mean if I win, you have to answer my questions?" Jas asked, looking at him from under her lashes.

"Sure," he replied nonchalantly, but his neck turned pink.

"Then it's a deal." Immediately, Jas wondered why she was accepting his challenge. When she was at the detention center, she'd played poker until she was sick of it. She'd gotten pretty good at winning, but what if she lost tonight?

I just won't lose.

Taking the cards from Chase, Jas dealt them out, snapping them down on the seat of the swing. "We'll play poker. Seven Card No Peek. Deuces wild."

Chase dragged one foot, slowing the swing.

"My favorite game," he said, turning over a two and a queen when she'd finished dealing. "Pair of queens."

Jas swallowed hard. As she turned over her cards, her palms began to sweat. After her sixth card, she had only a pair of threes.

Come on, deuce. Come on, three.

Slowly, she flipped over the last card—a ten. Her heart flew into her throat.

Chase rubbed his hands together gleefully. "Gee, I won. I guess that means I get to ask the first question."

Yes, I like you, Chase, and that's all I'm going to say.

"Why did you stab that Robicheaux guy?"

Jas was taken aback, even though she should have known he would ask about the assault. Maybe that's why she accepted the bet. Because a part of her wanted, almost *needed*, to confide in him.

"Why do you want to know about that?"

"Because I'm nosy," he joked. Then his expression turned serious. "No, I'd like to find out what you're hiding. And it obviously has something to do with that Robicheaux guy."

Jas tensed. Carefully, she weighed his words. Should she tell him? And if she did, would he help her?

She knew she needed help. There was no way she could get Hugh alone. Maybe this was too-perfect timing.

Angling her chin toward Chase, she met his gaze. The swing was rocking slowly, and his face moved in and out of the shadows. He met her eyes, and just when she thought her pounding heart would burst, she blurted, "I stabbed him because he killed Whirlwind."

He didn't even blink. "Well, shoot me. That's a great reason to stab somebody," he said. He smiled so goofily that it made Jas laugh with relief.

"So how do you know for sure that he killed the horse?" Chase asked, leaning forward as he shuffled the cards.

Jas snatched the deck from him. "I knew you wouldn't believe me."

"I do believe you," he declared. "I'm just playing cop. You know, finding out the evidence."

"Okay," Jas relented as she dealt the cards. "But asking me how I know he killed my horse will be your second question."

"Oh, right. Deal the cards so I can win again."

This time she won the hand with three aces. "Ooh," she crowed with delight. "Now I get to discover *your* deep, dark secrets."

He snorted. "No such thing. Mine are all shallow and bright."

"I'll have to think of something really good to ask." Jas chewed on her lip, dragging it out, wanting to keep him squirming.

Then it hit her what she had to ask him, and her smile slid from her face. Shivering, as if the summer air had grown chilly, she set her arm on the back of the swing and turned toward him. She was so nervous, she could feel her pulse beating in her wrists.

He slanted his eyes at her, and she could see the moon reflected in his pupils. She parted her lips, wanting to ask her question, but it stuck in her throat.

"What do you want to ask me?" His voice was so low it sounded like the wind rustling through the leaves.

"Can I..." She hesitated. "Can I trust you, Chase? I mean *totally* trust you?"

He cocked one brow so slightly she wasn't sure it had moved. Then slowly, he nodded. Reaching out, he brushed the back of her hand with his finger.

"Trust me, Jas. You need to trust somebody."

"I know," she whispered, relief flooding through her. And then she told him *everything*.

Chapter 18

"Do you think this will work?" Jas hollered from the floor of the backseat of Lucy's car.

"Of course not," Chase said. He was sitting in the front, and all she could see was the back of his head. "This is truly a boneheaded idea. James Bond would never—"

"Oh, who needs James Bond," Lucy cut in impatiently. She was driving, her long hair draped over the seat. "We're just breaking into some rich old guy's office. And if the dude shows up, I'll just have to distract him. I'm good at distracting men."

Jas rolled her eyes. If there'd been any other way, Jas would have never brought Lucy in on the plan to heist the photo album from High Meadows. But since neither she nor Chase could drive, they'd decided they had no choice.

Fortunately, Lucy bought the story that Jas had to sneak onto the farm to retrieve some personal things. And Miss Hahn had bought the story that they were going to the Bit and Bridle tack shop.

Since Hugh had a strict feeding schedule, Jas knew no one would be at the barn until five-thirty that evening. So Jas's challenge was to get in and out of his office and back to Miss Hahn's before lockdown at six—without getting caught.

"Anybody want some gum?" Lucy asked.

"Yeah, toss me a piece," Jas called. "I'm getting dog hair in my mouth."

"That's cat hair," said Lucy. "My two Siamese babies ride with me all the time."

"Here." Leaning over the seat, Chase dropped a chunk of bubble gum on Jas's chest, then grinned.

"Gee, thanks," she grumbled, but couldn't help but smile back.

"You don't look much like a criminal," Chase said, his chin propped on his hand as he looked down at her.

"Just wait until you see me shoot my way into Hugh's office. I'll be as ruthless as Jesse James." Unwrapping the gum, she stuck it in her mouth.

"So, Chase, what was it you promised me in return for this little favor?" Lucy purred.

Jas stopped in mid-chew.

Chase snapped his head around. "Uh, um, did

I promise you something?" he croaked.

Lucy burst out laughing. "You are so gullible. Face it, you're too young for me. You're more some cute JV cheerleader's type. Right, Jas?"

"Right, Lucy," Jas replied dryly. If Lucy hadn't been driving, Jas would have stuck her gum all over her hair.

"Hey, is this the place?" Lucy hollered. "High Meadows Farm?"

"Yeah, this is it."

Lucy whistled. "Woo-wee. How rich *is* this guy? His sign is bigger than my living room."

Jas was too nervous to answer. Frantically, she chewed her gum, and when she felt the car slow into the driveway, chills raced up her arms.

Chase cracked his knuckles. "Oh, boy. Here we go. And if we get caught, we don't even have weapons to defend ourselves."

Lucy made a scoffing noise. "Like you'd know how to shoot a gun. Ha!" She whistled again. "So how rich did you say this guy was?"

Jas figured they must be driving past Hugh's mansion. "Will you just get us to the barn, Lucy!" Jas hissed.

"All right. All right," Lucy grumbled. A minute later, the car stopped.

Chase peered at Jas over the seat. "It doesn't look like anybody's around."

Jas sat up. "Good. Come with me and be the lookout."

Lucy opened her door. "I'll mosey around, pretending I have enough money to buy one of Mr. Moneybags' horses."

"Mr. Robicheaux," Jas told her for the tenth time. "If somebody should come up, tell them you met Hugh at the Lexington Horse Center. And don't forget to keep whoever it is out of the barn."

"Right. I'm interested in one of his fifty-thousand-dollar show horses." Lucy slammed the door, and Jas heard the crunch of her sandals on the gravel as she walked away.

"All clear?" she asked Chase.

"Yeah." Chase got out and quickly opened the back door. Jas crawled out the side toward the barn. Then she stood, and the two made a run for it as Jas led the way.

From behind the barn came the shrill barking of the Jack Russells penned in their kennels. Jas had no idea who was caring for the horses while Hugh and Phil were gone. And since the terriers were making so much noise now, her fingers were crossed that the person wasn't staying on the farm.

She entered the barn through the open double doors, stopping in the wide aisleway. The horses were in for the day. Over the whir of the fans, she could hear their familiar snuffles and snorts. One horse whinnied, and for a second, Jas couldn't move. She hadn't realized how hard it would be to come back.

She wanted to rush from stall to stall, patting every horse–Pete and Romeo and the weanlings and...

"Hey," Chase whispered hoarsely. "What are we standing here for?"

Come on Jas, pull yourself together.

"Right, let's get going." She grabbed his hand and pulled him down the aisle to the tack room. The door was closed but not locked. They darted inside.

"Wow," Chase said as he stopped in the middle of the room. The tack room was paneled with dark mahogany plywood and smelled of leather and saddle soap. A dozen saddles and bridles hung from the walls above several tack trunks with HIGH MEADOWS FARM inscribed on their fronts. "This place is awesome."

Jas knew he had to be impressed. Not only was the barn gorgeous, but Hugh only bought the best. "How rich *is* this guy?" he echoed Lucy.

"Rich." Jas gestured to a door on the right. "There's the office. It's always locked."

"So how are you planning to break in?"

"The key."

Crouching by an antique hitching post, she tipped it up and felt underneath. She was out of luck if Hugh had moved the key.

Her fingers closed over the jagged metal. "It's here!"

"Good. I'll keep watch." Pulling his cap brim low, Chase slunk to the tack-room door and peered dramatically around the door frame. If Jas hadn't been so nervous, she would have burst out laughing.

She unlocked the office door, then carefully replaced the key under the hitching post. After opening the door, she stood in the doorway, unable to move. She'd been in the office a thousand times, and now it felt as if she'd never left.

Ribbons and photos covered the wall behind the polished walnut desk. Silver trophies gleamed from the shelf on the right. A file cabinet and bookshelves sat against the third wall.

Walking around the desk, Jas stared up at a framed photo of her and Whirlwind at the Columbia Horse Show last spring. She was mounted on Whirlwind, grinning at the camera, her hand caressing the mare's glossy neck. They'd been so triumphant that day. Now, three months later, it was nothing more than a forgotten dream.

A lump filled Jas's throat. Glancing away, she blinked back the tears. She had to hurry and find that album.

Grandfather had told her where it would probably be. She hoped Hugh hadn't moved it.

Jas kneeled next to the shelf by the file cabinet. The album was on top of a stack of books. Pulling it out, she tucked it under her arm and hurried from the office, pressing in the lock button on the doorknob before shutting the door.

"Jas! Someone's coming!" Wheeling away from the open door, Chase bounded toward her. From the horrified expression on his face, she knew he wasn't kidding.

"Who?"

"I don't know. I just heard a noise that sounded like someone was coming down the barn aisle. I ducked back so whoever it was wouldn't see me."

Jas clapped a hand over her mouth, suppressing a cry of panic. Her mind raced.

We've got to hide.

Jas grabbed Chase's wrist and dragged him to the office door. Bending, she set the album on the floor and snatched up the key from under the hitching post. She sprang to her feet, but a noise outside the tack-room door made her freeze.

"Too late," Chase whispered from behind her.

Slowly, Jas looked toward the doorway, the key clutched tightly in her hand.

Clink, clink. The person was almost at the door, jingling as if he had keys in his pocket. *Puff, huff, aaah.* The person sounded old and wheezy.

The new caretaker, Jas thought.

What could she tell him? What would she say that would keep him from telling Hugh or Phil?

Terrified, Jas stepped backward, bumping into Chase's chest. He put his hands on her shoulders and squeezed reassuringly.

"I'll tell whoever it is that it's all my fault," he said into her ear. "That I kidnapped you and brought you here."

Jas twisted her head to look at him. "You'd do that for—" she started to whisper, but his look of surprise cut her off.

"Oh, my!" Chase gasped. "An attack dog!"

Jas swung her head around. In the doorway stood a huge German shepherd.

"Sam!" she screeched as she tore across the tack room. Falling to the floor, she threw her arms around the old dog's neck. Tears poured down her cheeks. "Oh, Sam! It's you! Danvers said they were going to put you to sleep."

Whining and wiggling deliriously, Sam licked her face. Jas couldn't stop crying. She buried her head in the ruff of his neck. Fur stuck to her cheeks and lips, but she didn't care.

"That's your dog?" Chase asked as he came closer, the album in his hands.

"Yes. That barbarian Hugh told Danvers he was going to put him down. I can't believe he's all right." Standing, she slid her hand under his collar. "I'm taking him with me."

Chase opened his mouth to protest.

"He's Grandfather's dog, so it's not really stealing, and if I leave him, Hugh *will* have him put to sleep."

"You're right. Now let's get out of here before somebody does come."

Jas replaced the key. Then sticking her head out the doorway, she looked up and down the aisle. Part of her longed to stay and see all the horses, but she knew there was no way. Besides, she had to face it. Never again would High Meadows Farm be a part of her life.

"Come, Sam," she called as she sprinted out the door and down the barn aisle. But she didn't need to call him. Tail wagging, he trotted stiffly after her.

Lucy met them at the car. "What happened to you?" she asked, staring at Jas. "You look like a dog sat on your face."

"I was kissing one." Before Lucy could say anything else, Jas opened the back car door. Sam hopped in, dragging his arthritic back legs after him.

"The *dog* was the personal thing you had to get from the farm?" Lucy asked as she climbed into the driver's seat.

Jas draped her arm over Sam. "One of the things." Sliding in beside her, Chase shut the door.

"We made it!" Chase said, exhaling a huge sigh of relief.

When she started the motor, Lucy looked at the three of them crammed in the backseat. "While you two are back there grinning like fools, you better figure out what to tell Miss Hahn about the dog."

"Right," said Jas, but her mind was on the photo. Taking the album from Chase, she set it on her legs. Slowly, without breathing, she opened the heavy book. Beside her, Chase watched as Jas flipped through the pages of photos and newspaper and magazine articles. Hugh and his horses had appeared in countless newspapers and equine publications.

Halfway through the album, Jas found Aladdin's name underlined in a list of show results dated five years ago. He'd won the Columbia Open Jumper Cup.

"There's got to be a picture of him somewhere," Jas whispered, her pulse quickening.

Then she found it. A professional shot of Hugh jumping the big horse over a wall at the National Horse Show in New York.

Like Shadow, Aladdin was a handsome chestnut. His ears were pricked, his legs tucked to his chest as he cleared the wall with a foot to spare. Jas recognized the same sassy expression, the same devilish gleam in his eyes.

And the same exclamation point of white on his face.

Stunned, she glanced up at Chase. He was staring back at her, his lips forming a silent "wow." She knew that he knew, too.

Aladdin and Shadow were the same horse.

Chapter 19

"What are you guys looking at?" Lucy asked.

Startled, Jas shut the album. "Uh, just my old baby pictures."

"O-o-kay," Lucy said, though she didn't sound convinced.

Opening the album back up, Jas stared at the picture of Aladdin. The two horses were identical. But how could they be the same? Aladdin was dead! And yet if they *weren't* the same, who could explain the similar behavior and looks?

"What do you think?" Chase whispered.

Jas shook her head. "I don't know what to think."

Lucy glanced at them over her shoulder, swerving onto the grass. "What *are* you guys whispering about?"

Jas shut the album. "Nothing."

Tonight, she'd have to study the album carefully. On Wednesday, she'd take it in to show her grandfather. Only he would know what to do.

"I was just telling Chase how I wish I could've stayed to see all the horses," Jas fibbed.

"That Hugh guy does have some gorgeous animals," Lucy said as she stopped at the end of the drive, then turned left. "Do you think he needs someone to work for him? Since you were 'kindly asked to stay off the property,' he must need another rider."

Jas bit back a grin. She could picture Lucy bouncing wildly on one of Hugh's elegant Thoroughbreds. "Sure, go see him, Lucy. He'll love you."

"To death," Chase added in a mysterious voice, and Lucy shot him a funny look in the rearview mirror.

Jas held back a giggle. Chase reached for her hand, twining his fingers with hers. On Jas's other side, Sam flopped down, squashing his huge furry butt against the door handle and resting his head on her legs. His big eyes, cloudy with cataracts, gazed contentedly up at her as she stroked his graying muzzle.

"We'll tell Miss Hahn we found Sam hanging around garbage cans at the tack shop, looking very old and hungry," Jas said.

"Good idea," Lucy said. "She's a sucker for lost dogs."

"Only you better get rid of his collar."

Reaching across Jas's lap, Chase unbuckled Sam's collar. When they turned down a narrow road, he rolled down the car window.

"Wait, I want to do it." Jas took the collar from him and, leaning forward, threw it out.

The collar sailed through the air, the tags jingling. Turning in the seat, Jas watched until it landed and disappeared in the weeds.

"Are you sure you're ready to jump him?" Chase asked Jas the next day as he set up a crossbar in the middle of the paddock. "You've only ridden him three times."

Jas nodded as she steered Shadow past the bales of hay and two poles they were calling a jump. "He's been perfect. Besides, we need to see if he was professionally trained—by a jerk named Hugh Robicheaux."

Chase stood back to inspect the crossbar. It was only about two feet high in the middle. "I guess even old Sam could jump over this."

As Jas gathered the reins, her heart began to pound excitedly. It was the first time she'd jumped a horse in over six weeks.

But that wasn't the only reason she was excited.

She wanted to find out if Shadow's clearing the paddock fence was just a fluke. If the big horse couldn't jump worth a hoot, she knew there was no way he could be Aladdin.

"Say cheese!" Chase called when she rode by. He'd lifted up the camera that was hanging around his neck and was holding it to one eye. Sam was sprawled by his feet.

When they brought Sam back to the farm, Miss Hahn hadn't even questioned their story about finding him at the tack shop. She happily fed the shepherd a dog cookie, then told Jas and Chase to give him a flea bath.

This morning, Miss Hahn had left early for a meeting. As soon as she'd left, Jas had tacked up Shadow, figuring she could ride him before her lockdown time and Miss Hahn returned.

"Don't forget to take a shot of Shadow jumping so we can compare it to the photo in the album," Jas said, circling the big horse around the hay bales.

Even though Shadow was huge, his trot was light and springy, and he responded to Jas like a dream.

"I love this horse," she exclaimed as she thundered past Chase.

Jas trotted Shadow, keeping him slow and steady, and when the beat of his gait became as rhythmic as a song, she steered him down the middle. His ears tilted forward. His nose went up just enough so Jas knew he was focused and ready.

Without breaking stride, he jumped the crossbar, landed softly, then continued trotting. Grinning happily, Jas scratched his withers. He shook his head as if to say, "Was that all?"

"He just stepped over the thing," Chase said in amazement. "Keep trotting while I put it up to three feet."

When Chase had adjusted the poles, Jas again turned Shadow toward the jump. He trotted over it, his back rounding in a perfect bascule.

Chase hooted. "Four feet!"

"No way!" Jas shot back, but already he was adjusting the fence, dragging another hay bale to make it higher. "Three feet six," she said. "I'll pretend it's a fence in one of my junior hunter classes."

Even though Jas had jumped the height a hundred times, her mouth went dry. This time, she cantered Shadow down the center, keeping light contact on the reins. He didn't tug or rush. When he leaped the bales as if they weren't even there, her heart leaped with him.

He landed on the other side, ducked his head, and bucked playfully. Jas was too excited to scold him. Halting at the end of the paddock, she dropped her reins and threw her arms around his sweaty neck. "You were terrific!"

"He cleared it by two feet!" Chase whooped as he jogged over, Sam trailing behind him. "Just like the other day when he jumped out–"

Jas straightened just as Miss Hahn came walking over, the burros ambling alongside. She shot Chase a horrified look. He clamped his mouth shut, but it was too late.

"When he did what?" Miss Hahn demanded as she opened the gate and came into the paddock. "And why are you jumping that horse without asking me first?"

"Uh-h-h," Chase sputtered.

Crossing her arms, Miss Hahn waited for an answer.

"We wanted to surprise you?" Chase guessed.

Jas was too afraid to speak. Miss Hahn had obviously seen Shadow jump. If Shadow *was* Aladdin, there was a good chance she would recognize him.

Quickly, Jas searched for an explanation that would keep Miss Hahn from getting too suspicious. "Uh, last Saturday, Shadow jumped out of the paddock," she said, which was the truth.

Miss Hahn's jaw dropped. "Over the paddock fence? But that's five feet high."

"I know. Chase and I decided that he was probably trained as a jumper. So we wanted to try him out." She dropped her gaze. "I'm sorry we didn't tell you first," she added contritely, hoping Miss Hahn would buy it.

For a minute, Miss Hahn frowned at the two of them, as if disappointed they hadn't told her. Then she shrugged. "Well, I guess nothing was hurt. You better cool Shadow off. Though, judging by that last buck, he's not hot or tired. When he gets in shape, we'll take him over to my friend Lydia's and let him see some real fences."

As if he knew she was talking about him, Shadow rubbed his face against Miss Hahn's arm. She patted him on the head. "You know, when I saw him jump, it occurred to me that I've seen him before. I wonder if he was originally from around here?"

Jas inhaled sharply. With a horrified expression, she looked at Chase. *Don't say anything,* she mouthed.

This morning, Shadow proved that he *was* a jumper, just like Aladdin. It could still be a coincidence, so Jas had lots more sleuthing to do. Having Chase know what she was up to had been risky. But if Miss Hahn guessed something was going on, it would blow everything.

⚜

"Grandfather, I want you to meet Chase," Jas said on Sunday's visit. She stood behind his wheelchair ready to take him out to the patio.

"Ase?" Craning his neck like an old turtle, Grandfather inspected Chase from head to toe. Chase stood by the bed, his baseball cap in one hand, looking awkward. "Kind of ittle and kinny, ain't he?"

"He says you're tall and handsome," Jas said when Chase gave her a puzzled look. "Ready to go outside?" she asked as she pushed the wheelchair out of the room and down the hall.

"I'm ready to get *out*," Grandfather grumbled. The stronger he felt, the more he chafed at being at the nursing home.

"I know," Jas said. "It won't be long."

As they walked down the hall, Chase strode beside Jas, casting uneasy looks at the old people shuffling into the rec room for Bingo. Grandpa grunted as they passed by. "I ate ingo."

"Then it's good we came when we did." Turning the chair around, Jas went backward through the double doors that led outside. Then she pushed Grandfather onto the brick patio and over to a bench under a tree.

"Ahhhh." Closing his eyes, he laid his head against the back of the wheelchair and breathed deeply. Jas took the album from Chase and set it on Grandfather's lap. Then she flipped through until she found Aladdin's picture. From his pocket, Chase pulled the Polaroid of Shadow that he'd taken the day before and set it next to the photo of Aladdin. Then they waited, sitting side by side on the bench, their knees touching, while Grandfather studied the pictures.

"So wasn't I right?" Jas said. Yesterday, she had told Grandfather everything on the phone.

He nodded as he turned the page to the newspaper article about Aladdin's death. Last night, Jas had pored over the article, trying to find some clue. Just like Phil had said, Aladdin had died of colic five years ago—right in the middle of an outstanding jumping career.

"Twins," Grandfather finally said.

"That's what Chase and I thought. They're even the right ages," Jas explained. "Aladdin was seven when he supposedly died five years ago. Danvers said Shadow's about twelve."

Chase tapped the photo of Aladdin. "But we can't figure out how they could be the same horse."

"A inger," Grandfather declared.

"What?" Jas leaned forward to hear him better.

"A r-inger," he repeated.

"A ringer?" Jas knew what a ringer was from stories about double-dealing on the racetrack. It was a horse that looked identical to another horse. "You mean Shadow is a ringer for Aladdin?"

"Es." Grandfather pressed his mouth in a line. Turning the pages, he hunted through the album. When he found two photos, he tapped them wildly. "Here! This explains it! Afer Uhaddin ied Hugh ought ese oo orses or over a illion ollars!" He spat the words so fast that Jas didn't have a clue what he was saying.

She looked closer at the photos. They showed Hugh holding his stallion Whirligig, who had sired Whirlwind. After standing him for two years, he'd sold him to a syndicate.

The other picture was of a Thoroughbred yearling Hugh had bought at the auction in Kentucky. He'd cost over half a million dollars, but went bust as a racehorse.

"Don't oo see?" Grandfather declared, clutching at Jas's arm.

"No. You've got to slow down."

He took a deep breath, then started again, enunciating each word. "After Uhaddin died, Hugh spent over a million on two horses. But he only got twenty-five ousand from Uhaddin's insurance money."

"But Hugh's rich."

Grandfather swung his head. "Not that rich. And ee spends everything he makes."

Puzzled, Jas tried to understand what Grandfather was saying. Grandfather grasped her wrist with bony fingers and pulled her even closer.

"What if Hugh didn't kill Uhaddin?" he whispered. "What if ee killed a ringer?"

Jas's eyes widened as she slowly understood what Grandfather was saying. Beside her, Chase sucked in his breath as if he got it, too.

"You mean Hugh killed a horse that looked like Aladdin, but wasn't Aladdin," Jas said, repeating what she thought he was trying to say. "But since everyone thought he was Aladdin, Hugh collected the insurance money. At the same time, he sold the *real* Aladdin, who by then was worth a lot of money!"

"The creep would have collected twice!" Chase exclaimed.

"But Aladdin was pretty well known by then," Jas pointed out. "So how'd Hugh get away with it? I mean, first, he had to find a horse that looked like Aladdin. Then he had to sell the real Aladdin. Only he couldn't just sell the horse to anybody, because someone would have recognized him."

Grandfather winked. "South America."

"You mean Hugh sold the horse overseas?"

"Ight. They buy lots of orses. No questions asked."

"Wow." Jas slumped back on the bench. It all made sense—almost. "Then if Shadow is the real Aladdin, how did he get back to Virginia?"

Grandfather shrugged. "The new owners didn't want him anyor when he got sick," he guessed, his voice growing fainter and less clear.

Jas could tell he was getting tired. "Rest a minute," she said, patting his knee.

Leaning his head back, Grandfather closed his eyes. Jas took the album and set it on Chase's legs.

"If Hugh's the conniving sleaze you say he is," Chase said in a low voice, "then your grand-father's explanation makes perfect sense."

"It does make sense. The article says Aladdin died in the middle of an impressive first season on the jumping circuit. His value was skyrocket-ing, but he was just starting to attract attention in the horse world. It would have been the perfect time to arrange his death."

"Any later and Aladdin would have been too famous," Chase agreed. But then he frowned. "Only, why did a well-known guy like Hugh take the chance? Killing your horse isn't a crime. But insurance fraud is. Hugh had to know he'd get in serious trouble if he was caught."

Jas arched one brow. "*If* he was caught. And he wasn't. Obviously no one discovered that the dead horse wasn't Aladdin."

A sudden memory made Jas shudder. "And I can understand why. I remember how different Whirlwind looked when she was lying there—" Jas's voice cracked. "And now that I know Hugh better," Jas went on, feeling more anger now than sadness, "I realize he enjoys the risks almost as much as the money. Otherwise, why would he have called me up and used Aladdin's name in the first place?"

Without opening his eyes, Grandfather chuckled. "Yup. Oo nailed it, Jas. Hugh is a crafty devil." Opening one eye, he tapped himself on the temple. "But not as mart and crafty as you and me! We'll get Hugh. Don't oo worry."

But Jas wasn't as confident as Grandfather. If Aladdin was Shadow, then Hugh had gotten away with a really devious scheme.

"Hey, don't look so glum," Chase said. "We'll figure this out."

"I'm glad you and Grandfather are optimistic," Jas said, sighing gloomily. "Because even though we think we've figured it all out, the reality is—we don't have a shred of proof."

Chapter 20

"You're right about needing more proof, Jas," Chase said after breakfast the next morning. "We're only *guessing* that Hugh scammed his insurance company."

They were carrying a bale of hay out to the shed in the back pasture. The weather had been so dry that the grass had quit growing.

"I know," Jas said, feeling discouraged. She dropped the bale when they reached the shed. Chase pulled a Swiss Army knife from his back pocket and cut the twine. Then they threw the hay into the rack. Already, the four horses who shared the field had ambled into the shed and were grabbing mouthfuls of hay that had fallen to the ground.

"Hey, Spots." Jas scratched the pinto on his fat neck. "I heard you're being adopted this weekend."

"A family with twin daughters. He'll definitely get lots of TLC."

Jas smiled sadly. "That's nice. Only…"

"You'll miss the ugly plug?" Chase guessed. Picking up the twine, he wound it into a ball, then stuck it in his pocket.

She nodded.

"That seems hard to believe considering you're such a horse snob," he teased.

"Oh, shut up." Jas threw the last section of hay at him. He ducked and it hit Spots, who snorted and bolted from the shed.

"Stampede!" Chase joked as he ran from the shed with the horse. Jas raced him to the barn, and they collapsed on the bales in the aisle, completely out of breath. Sam came up, his tongue hanging, and flopped down on top of Jas's feet.

"So where are we going to get proof?" Jas asked. Leaning back on his elbows, Chase stretched his long legs in front of him. "How about Phil or Danvers? They're probably the only ones besides Hugh who really knew Aladdin."

"There's also Reaves. He knows where Shadow came from."

"Reaves? Hah. He'd never tell the truth."

"Well, Phil's out, that's for sure."

Chase pulled a stalk of hay from the bale and stuck it between his lips. "Then it's Danvers. And you're in luck," he said with a twinkle in his blue eyes. "He's coming over for dinner tonight."

"A big date, huh?"

Chase nodded, and they both giggled.

"Well, that's good. Before dinner, I'll show Danvers the album. You can keep Miss Hahn occupied in the kitchen."

"Hmm." He wrinkled his forehead as if absorbed in deep thought. "I could drop the salad on the floor."

Jas laughed. "I knew you'd be a good partner in crime."

Pulling the hay from between his lips, Chase held it between two fingers like a cigarette. "Just call me Bond," he said in a British accent. "James Bond."

That night, Jas wore the only dress she owned. It was made of a soft, clingy fabric. The skirt was short, showing off her now tan and muscular legs. When she came down the steps barefoot, Chase's eyes widened in surprise.

"Um...what happened to your jeans?" he asked.

"Never mind." Linking her arm with his, she steered him away from the kitchen door. "Is Danvers here?"

"In the kitchen, standing *very* close to Miss Hahn, tasting spaghetti sauce."

"Okay. Here's the plan." She lowered her

voice. "Call him into the living room for something. I'll run up and get the album."

Chase nodded with utmost seriousness. "And I'll drop the salad."

"Right." He was bent slightly to hear her, and without warning, he suddenly angled his head and kissed her. When he pulled back, he was grinning like a little kid. "Sorry. I couldn't help myself. It's all this intrigue."

"Right, it's the intrigue," Jas repeated, too surprised to say anything else. Her heart was beating like a drum, and when he went into the kitchen, she thumped up the steps, touching her lips. *Did he really just kiss me?*

As she came down, Jas heard a loud crash from the kitchen, then, "Oh, gee, sorry, Miss Hahn. I'm as clumsy as a horse wearing high heels."

"You wanted to see me?" Danvers asked. Jas could barely recognize him. He was sitting on the sofa sipping iced tea, wearing khakis and a short-sleeved shirt, instead of his baggy coveralls.

"Yes. Now, I know you and Phil vowed to drop the whole Whirlwind thing, and this isn't about her. Well, it sort of is, but I don't want you to cut me off until I show you everything."

"*Phil* said *he* wasn't going to pursue the matter anymore," Danvers corrected her. "I just ran out of time and energy."

Hope fluttered in Jas's chest as she sat down next to him. Maybe he *would* help. "It's about Aladdin," she told him. Opening the album, she showed him the picture and the article.

"Yeah, I remember him," Danvers said. "Hugh was crushed when the horse died."

"So crushed that he immediately ran out and bought two horses worth a million dollars," Jas said sarcastically.

Danvers was about to take another drink, but he lowered his glass. "What?"

"Grandfather and I have this theory." Leaning closer, she told him their idea.

Danvers frowned. "So what you're saying is Hugh killed some horse that looked like Aladdin and collected the insurance money? Then sold the real Aladdin somewhere overseas for big bucks?"

Jas nodded excitedly.

Danvers hunched forward, his frown deepening. "I hope you haven't told anyone else this wild idea of yours, Jas."

Her excitement faded. "Why?"

"Because you're making a serious and unfounded accusation. Hugh could really make trouble for you."

Jas pressed her lips together. "You're on his side, too! I should have known not to trust you."

She stood up, catching the album before it fell off her lap.

Grasping her wrist to stop her, Danvers spoke in a tense voice. "This has nothing to do with trust, young lady. This has to do with the facts. Hugh bought Aladdin from Holland and had him imported. Most European horses have a computer microchip implanted in their necks for identification. When Aladdin died, I used a scanner to check his microchip number. The horse that died of colic five years ago *was* Aladdin."

Stunned by what he was saying, Jas sank down onto the sofa. "That can't be! Because Aladdin is *here*, in Miss Hahn's barn."

Danvers's woolly eyebrows shot up. "What?"

"Shadow *is* Aladdin."

"Jas. Get a grip. Aladdin *died*. There's no way Hugh could have faked that microchip."

"No way?" Jas croaked. "Couldn't he have taken the chip out—"

"No!" Danvers said firmly. "Once they're implanted in the neck, they're almost impossible to remove. And it would be just as impossible to reinsert it in another horse's neck."

Jas fell back against the sofa pillows, drained. If what Danvers said was true, then her whole idea about Shadow *was* just an obsession. Hugh must have thrown out the horse's name to divert her from digging into Whirlwind's death.

But she wasn't giving up yet. She had one more idea to run by Danvers. "So if Shadow by some wild chance is Aladdin...he would still have that microchip in his neck, right?"

Setting down his glass, Danvers threw his hands in the air. "I give up. What is it going to take to get you to drop this nutty idea?"

"Easy. Use your scanner tonight to see if there's a microchip in Shadow's neck."

Danvers blew out a breath of frustration. "Jas, that's crazy. There's one chance in a million, no, a *billion*, that what you're saying is true."

"And what if by some chance I'm right?" she countered.

Danvers scowled at her, then threw up his hands again. "Okay, I give up. I'll scan Shadow's neck tonight."

"Yes!" Jas punched the air with her fist.

"But even if he has a microchip, that doesn't mean he's Aladdin. I'll have to find my old file on Aladdin to see if the numbers match up. Once a horse dies, his number is deleted from the national registry."

"Thank you." Jas beamed at him.

"Promise me one thing, though," he said sternly.

"What?"

"We get to eat dinner first." He patted his stomach. "The spaghetti sauce tasted terrific."

Jas grinned. "And just wait until you taste the salad!"

"Chase, you're going to have to get Shadow and bring him into the yard," Jas said as they stood side by side at the sink, washing dishes after dinner.

"Why me?" he asked, then immediately answered his own question. "Oh, right—lockdown time."

"I can't go into the barn this late with this stupid thing on my ankle." Annoyed, she kicked at her leg.

Chase dried his hands on a dish towel. "What are you going to tell Miss Hahn?"

"How about if you ask her to take you home. That will get rid of her. I don't want her snooping around."

"Why not?"

"I have my reasons."

"Okay, only promise you'll call me later and tell me what happened."

"It's a deal." She smiled shyly at him, knowing that once they got on the phone, they would talk forever. Jas couldn't remember ever having a friend like Chase. Then she remembered the kiss, and a warm flush spread up her neck.

"Miss Hahn!" Chase hollered into the living room. "I gotta get home."

"Now?" Miss Hahn asked.

"I have to be home by, uh, seven-thirty," he fibbed.

Miss Hahn sighed. "Oh, all right."

"Now quick," Jas hissed as she finished drying a plate. "Run and get Shadow. I'll meet you at the gate."

Chase threw her the dish towel, then bounded from the kitchen.

Jas busied herself with the dishes. "He'll meet you out by the van," she told Miss Hahn ten minutes later when she came in with her purse and car keys. Danvers was right behind her.

"Dr. Danvers, while they're gone, could you check Shadow's leg for me? I think it was puffy from jumping the other day. Chase is bringing him around."

"In the dark?" Miss Hahn said, but then Chase yelled "woo-hoo" from the backyard, and she hurried out the door.

Jas dried her hands, slipped on her sneakers, and followed them out. Shadow stood in the light from the back porch, his head up and eyes glowing. Chase was hopping on one foot.

"Hey, big boy, it's all right," Jas soothed as she crossed the lawn.

"It's not all right," Chase grumbled. "The big clod stepped on my foot."

"I wasn't talking to you." Jas yanked the lead from his hand. "Would you get her out of here?" she said, pointing to Miss Hahn.

Still grimacing, he hobbled after Miss Hahn, mumbling, "If I knew detective work was going to be this hard..."

Jas let Shadow graze while she waited for Danvers to get the scanner from his pickup. The big horse's ears flicked at the unfamiliar sight of an electronic scanner. When Danvers came up holding it, he snorted anxiously.

"It transmits a radio signal to the microchip," Danvers explained to Jas as he turned it on and began passing it over Shadow's neck. Pinning his ears, the big horse danced sideways.

Jas shortened her hold on the lead and reassured him with a massage on his withers. "You're all right, you big baby."

"If there's a microchip in his neck, it will signal its number back to the reader. You'll see it here on this screen."

"Then you can compare the number to the one in Aladdin's file?"

"Right," Danvers said, giving her a doubtful look. "Though the odds are zero that it will match. And if he does have a number and it doesn't match, I'm going to have to call it in to the national registry. It may match another horse. Maybe one that was reported stolen."

"Oh." Jas's mouth went dry. She hadn't thought about that. What if Shadow belonged to someone else? Then she would probably have to give him back. Now she hoped more than ever that she was right.

"Hey! I've got a number," Danvers said, sounding surprised. "He does have a microchip."

He showed Jas the digits illuminated on the reader's screen. "I'll write it down. In the morning, I'll have my office assistant hunt up Aladdin's old file. I'll call you when I know something."

Jas nodded. When Danvers went back to his truck, she burrowed her nose in Shadow's mane and listened to the cropping noise he made as he tore at the grass.

Maybe she was making a big mistake. In her zeal to get Hugh, what if she lost Shadow? She'd already lost Whirlwind. She didn't think she could stand losing Shadow, too.

Chapter 21

The next morning, Jas gave Shadow a bath. "Hold still, you big gorilla," she scolded as she sponged water on his sweaty back. Shaking his head playfully, he switched his tail, then shook like a dog, spraying Jas with water.

It was already eleven o'clock, and Jas hadn't heard from Dr. Danvers. She'd phoned once, but he hadn't returned her call. The waiting was driving her crazy.

"Hey!" She jerked on Shadow's lead, and for a second he stood quietly. Then the geese burst from the barn, and with a snort of terror the big horse leaped in the air.

Jas gritted her teeth. She knew she should have ridden him for two hours this morning instead of one. Then she could have given him a really good workout. But she didn't want to miss Danvers's call, so she cut Shadow's workout short.

As Jas whisked the excess water off with a

sweat scraper, she studied Shadow from head to tail. He was so powerful and athletic. With the right training, he could turn into a winning jumper.

At least on Saturday, he would get a start. Miss Hahn was hauling Shadow to her friend Lydia's house so Jas could work him in her ring. Lydia had lots of money. Jas knew her reasonably well since she'd often come out to High Meadows Farm to look over Hugh's horses.

"Get out of here, you stupid birds!" Just then Chase charged from the barn, waving a broom at the geese. Pointing it like a rifle, he sighted it, then yelled, "Boom! Boom! Gotcha!"

With a snort, Shadow ran backward, knocking over the bucket. "Gee, thanks, Chase." Jas scowled as she picked up the bucket with one hand while trying to control her wild-eyed horse with the other.

"Sorry, but those stupid geese keep getting in the feed room. I think we should have a big goose supper this Christmas to raise money for the farm."

Jas laughed.

Chase grinned back at her. "That's nice to hear. You've been pretty grumpy all morning."

"Well, I can't stand waiting for Danvers's call. I mean, what if Shadow is someone else's horse?"

"Jas! Dr. Danvers is on the phone!" Lucy bellowed from the office.

Jas's stomach somersaulted. She thrust the lead at Chase. "Be right back."

She raced to the office. Lucy was holding on to the receiver, her hand covering the mouthpiece. Arching one brow, she stuck out her hip and looked curiously at Jas.

"He just wants to know if Shadow's leg is better," Jas fibbed. Taking the phone, she turned her back, took a breath to steady herself, and said, "Hello."

"I've got some bad news, Jas," Danvers said. "Shelly can't find Aladdin's old file anywhere. We may have thrown it out since the horse was deceased."

"Oh." Jas wasn't sure if she was relieved or dismayed.

"But don't give up. I'm going to contact the insurance company. They must still have it on file. You have definitely piqued my curiosity. So I'll let you know as soon as I find out something. But it may be a couple of days."

"That's fine." Slowly, Jas hung up. Lucy had left, and the office was empty. She slumped into one of the hard chairs. Sam came up the steps, his toenails clicking on the wood. With a woof of greeting, he laid his head on her thighs.

Bending, she kissed him on the muzzle, then dug her fingers into his ruff. "Sam, what if I'm making a huge mistake?" she said, echoing her thoughts from the other night. "What if Shadow has nothing to do with Hugh and I lose him?"

Except…

Jas stared out the office door, gnawing on her lip. Something was nagging at her. Something she couldn't put into words. There was another reason why she had to know if Aladdin and Shadow were the same horse. Sure, she wanted to nail Hugh, but something else was bothering her. Only, she couldn't quite get a hold of what it was. All she knew was that it had to do with Whirlwind. And it was *very* important.

She only hoped she could figure it out in time.

"No, don't worry. We're not going to the auction," Jas told Shadow on Saturday as she led him toward the ramp of the horse trailer. "We're going to Lydia's so I can work your butt off in her ring."

Hanging back, his front legs braced, the big horse looked as if he didn't believe a word she said.

"I don't think he wants to go in," Chase said, a grooming box in one hand and a bridle in the other.

"I don't know why. We practiced all this week, and he loaded like a dream."

"Yeah, but he knew you weren't going anywhere." Chase put the gear in the open truck bed. Then sticking his thumbs in his pockets, he rocked back on his boot heels and furrowed his brow as if he was assessing the situation. "Now that you've got protective wraps on him, he knows for sure something's going on."

Jas rolled her eyes. "Thank you, Dr. Chase, horse psychologist."

"Hey, just helping."

"Just helping would be getting me a bucket of feed, please."

"All right. All right."

Miss Hahn bustled from the office. "Trouble loading? Should I call Lydia and tell her we'll be late? She expects us in half an hour."

"No. Chase went to get grain. That should work." Letting the lead loose a little, Jas went up to Shadow. Tucking his head, he snuffled at her palm. "I think he expects something horrible to happen. Like a trip to the killers."

"Probably. People say horses don't think, but I disagree. And I know for sure they have a good memory." A strange expression passed over Miss Hahn's face, and she glanced hastily away as if afraid to meet Jas's eyes.

Jas clutched the lead rope, sensing that Miss Hahn was about to say something that Jas didn't want to hear.

Did she find out about Danvers looking for the microchip? Did she tell Hugh about it?

Jas took a deep breath, wondering how she was going to deal with this. She was too close to finding out the truth to let Miss Hahn ruin everything.

"Jas, while we're at Lydia's farm, she's going to be watching Shadow very closely," Miss Hahn said. "I know her and I know what kind of horse she likes. And this"—she nodded at Shadow—"is it."

No. Jas's lips formed the words, but she was so surprised, nothing came out.

Miss Hahn's brown eyes filled with sadness. "In three weeks, you'll have your probation hearing. Your grandfather's getting better, which means you'll soon be leaving us. I'd love for you to adopt Shadow, but you know that you and your grandfather will have enough to deal with without worrying about a hay-guzzling animal. Shadow's too healthy to stay here. Lydia would be wonderful for him, and he'd be wonderful for her."

Tears filled Jas's eyes. She knew Miss Hahn was right. She'd been so wrapped up in solving her mystery and in her dreams about Shadow that she'd totally forgotten the reality of her situation: Shadow wasn't her horse.

Miss Hahn touched Jas's shoulder. "I'm sorry." Her voice was thick, as if she was about to cry. "But I thought I better warn you before we go, in case Lydia says something."

Turning, she hurried to the truck. Jas watched her through blurry eyes. Chase bustled from the barn, whistling, a bucket swinging from one hand. Tipping his ears, Shadow whinnied at him.

"Okay, big boy, let's get you loaded." Taking the lead from Jas, he walked the horse right up the ramp and into the trailer.

Jas stood rooted to the spot, dazed. She'd been dreaming about Shadow being the next Junior Jumper Champion. Now it all seemed so shallow and stupid.

"*That's* how to load a horse, ladies!" Chase said triumphantly from inside the trailer.

The tears spilled over and rolled down Jas's cheeks.

The phone rang in the office, and Jas sprinted across the barnyard, needing to get away before she fell apart. "I'll get it," she yelled.

She grabbed the receiver and gasped, "Second Chance Farm."

"Jas, it's Dr. Danvers."

Jas's heart went into overdrive. *No. Not now. I*

*don't want to hear whatever it is you found out. I
can't take anymore.*

"You were right! Shadow's number matched
with Aladdin's. They're the same horse!"

Jas dropped the receiver. It banged hollowly
on the desktop, but she could still hear. Danvers
rattled on excitedly.

"I told the insurance guy. We've got a meeting
tomorrow to try and figure out how Hugh dupli-
cated the microchip and put it in the lookalike
horse that died..."

But Jas didn't want to hear the rest. Falling
against the door frame, she burst into sobs. She
buried her face in her hands, trying to shut out
Danvers's words. Because suddenly she realized
it didn't matter if they proved that Aladdin was
Shadow, and Hugh had scammed the insurance
company. It didn't even matter if they could tie it
to Whirlwind's death.

Because no matter how it all turned out, Jas
would lose.

Chapter 22

"I'll find out where she wants us to put Shadow," Miss Hahn said as she got out of the truck, which she parked in front of Lydia's barn.

Jas nodded. She hadn't been able to say a word the whole trip. She was too stunned.

"You all right?" Chase asked after Miss Hahn had gone.

Jas nodded, afraid to say anything. She didn't want to start crying all over again.

"What did Danvers tell you?"

"He said Aladdin and Shadow had the same microchip number," Jas said flatly.

"So they're the same horse!" Chase smacked his fist against his palm. "We were right!"

When Jas didn't say anything, he frowned. "Isn't that what you wanted, Jas? When the insurance company knows Aladdin's alive, they'll investigate Hugh. They should be able to get him for something illegal."

"I know," Jas choked out the words.

"Then what's wrong?"

Pulling up her knees, Jas wrapped her arms around her ankles, the fingers of her left hand hitting the transmitter. She'd worn her breeches, and the stretchy material felt cool to the touch. "I thought getting Hugh would make everything better. But it still won't bring Whirlwind back. And if Miss Hahn's friend, Lydia, likes Shadow, she's going to take him."

"She's what?" Chase shoved his baseball cap off his forehead. "That's not fair. He's *your* horse."

Jas shook her head. "No, he's not. Miss Hahn bought him."

"Well, then, when you ride today, knock down every jump. Then Lydia won't like him."

"Or even better, how about if I jump him out of the ring and trample Lydia," Jas said bitterly.

"There you go." Chase ran his finger lightly down her cheek. "I knew you wouldn't give up without a fight."

Jas sighed. "Except Miss Hahn's right. When Grandfather gets out of the nursing home, and I go to live with him, we'll be living in an apartment where I wouldn't be able to keep a horse."

Chase whistled. "Wow. I'd forgotten about that. I guess I thought you might still live at Second Chance Farm."

"Only I can't, Chase, you know that. Soon I

won't be a reject anymore." She tried to make it sound like a joke. "Someone will want me. My grandfather."

"Yeah? Well, someone already wants you."

When Jas looked at him, he reddened. "I mean, two someones and a horse," he added under his breath.

"You were right the first time. Miss Hahn never really wanted me. She took me in so she could spy on me for Hugh."

"Hugh?" Chase repeated. "Where'd you get that crazy idea?"

Jas waved her hand. "It's a long story."

"No, it's the *wrong* story," he argued. "I don't know what her initial reason was for taking you in, but I know that right now she really cares about you."

"Maybe." Jas shrugged. "But it doesn't really matter. When I have my court hearing in August, *everything* is going to change. And I won't have any control over it." She laid her chin on her knees. "It's really weird thinking back to the afternoon Whirlwind died. When I attacked Hugh, I had no idea it would change my life. I remember thinking before my trial that everything had been turned upside down. Now it's happening again."

A kick from the trailer made her jerk her

head up. "I guess we better unload Shadow."

"Okay, but this conversation isn't over," Chase said. "You're *not* leaving the farm and just disappearing from our lives."

Jas glanced sideways at him. *I won't,* she wanted to say. But she had no idea what would happen. "You guys getting out?" Miss Hahn rapped on the side window. "Lydia says to put Shadow in the empty stall in the barn. And Jas, you can borrow Lydia's saddle in the tack room. It'll probably fit him better than the old one you've been using."

"Thanks," Jas said, trying to muster a little enthusiasm.

"I'll unload Shadow and walk him around for a while to get the kinks out," Chase offered as he got out. "You get your stuff and I'll meet you at the stall."

"Okay." For a second, Jas looked out the windshield. Lydia's place was like a miniature High Meadows Farm. Horses and cattle grazed in emerald green pastures surrounded by white board fences. There was an indoor and outdoor ring, and even a cross-country course on the hillside.

How ironic, Jas thought. A few days ago, she was dying to live at a farm like Lydia's and try Shadow over a real course. Now all she wanted to do was take him back to Second Chance Farm.

Jas sighed as she slid across the seat and climbed from the truck. Miss Hahn and Lydia stood behind the trailer, waiting for Chase to unload Shadow.

Jas pulled her helmet from the truck bed. After tucking her hair behind her ears, she put it on. She pulled out the grooming box and Shadow's bridle. As she dragged herself into Lydia's barn, she felt she was moving in slow motion.

Maybe Chase is right. I should fight for Shadow. If I tried, I could make him look as crazy as a bronco. And if Lydia hates him, then at least I have him for a little while longer.

Feeling better, Jas hurried down the aisle until she came to what looked like the door to the tack room. Draping the bridle over her shoulder, she opened the door. The room was dark.

When she stepped inside, she groped along the wall for a light switch. She flicked it on, but nothing happened.

A thump from the far corner made her stiffen. Eyes wide, she stared into the dark room, her brain trying to make sense of the unfamiliar shapes. She could make out saddles and bridles. But then her gaze stopped at a larger, rounded form silhouetted against the back wall, as if a person was sitting on something.

"Hello?" she called, feeling foolishly scared.

"Hello, Jas."

The silky-smooth voice sent shivers up Jas's spine. The shape moved, and a boot clunked on the floor.

Hugh. Jas's fingers tightened around the handle of the grooming box. *No, this isn't happening,* she thought, fear rising in her throat. *Your mind is playing tricks.*

"Close the door behind you, Jas. We have a lot to talk about and we don't have much time."

Jas didn't move. Then she realized that no matter how scared she was, she needed to find out what he wanted. He wouldn't have risked being with her unless it was important.

Raising her foot, she kicked the door shut behind her, leaving it open a crack–just in case.

"What do you want?" she whispered.

"I hear you've been telling people that you have my horse."

He knows about Shadow! Anger flared inside her. "Did Miss Hahn tell you?" she demanded.

"It doesn't matter how I found out, Jas. What's important is that you tell me everything and that you give up this obsession."

"No! I won't give up." Jas glared fiercely at his dark shape. "Especially now. The insurance company knows you cheated them, and when they prosecute you, *you'll* find out what it feels like to be guilty."

Hugh exhaled, expressing his impatience. "Don't play dumb, Jas, because I know you're not. You were smart enough to discover some things that were better left alone. Now be smart enough to quit. The insurance company will never prosecute me. One of the clerks from the company is calling Danvers right now to explain that the company made a mistake and that the two horses' numbers do *not* match."

Jas sucked in her breath. "But...how...?"

"Power and money, Jas. They make things happen like that." He snapped his fingers.

"But Danvers knows," Jas protested. "And you won't be able to buy him off."

"The only thing Danvers knows is that his files on Aladdin are gone and he can't prove a thing. Don't make it harder than it already is," Hugh said. "In two weeks, you'll be free. I lived up to my deal, and your grandfather's received the best of care. As soon as he's strong and your probation is over, you two can start life over— somewhere far from Stanford and me."

He sounded so sane and reasonable that Jas almost nodded in agreement. But then the vision of Whirlwind, her eyes glazed over in death, filled her.

"Only you killed Whirlwind," Jas choked out. "And somehow, you're going to pay for it."

Hugh didn't say anything. Instead, he looked down at the ground, a devious smile planted on his face. The room grew so thick with silence that suddenly Jas knew the truth. She realized why it was important to figure out that Shadow and Aladdin were the same horse. She knew what her brain was trying to tell her all along.

Whirlwind wasn't dead!

Chapter 23

The dim light from the open doorway streamed across the room and sent a line of gray angling up to Hugh's face. Jas could see the gleam of his eyes.

"Whirlwind's not dead, is she?" Jas whispered. "You killed another horse. A ringer. Then you sold Whirlwind to someone else. Just like you did with Aladdin."

The light caught Hugh's arrogant smirk. "That's right. It took me a while to find her twin, almost a year of combing auctions. But I obviously did a good job since even you never suspected it wasn't her lying in that paddock."

"Where is she?" Jas demanded.

"She's safe. But you'll never find her, which means you'll never prove she's alive."

Abruptly, Jas straightened. "I don't care about proof anymore," she said. "You're evil, Hugh. You may not have killed Aladdin or Whirlwind, but you killed two other horses. Then you blamed

one of the deaths on my grandfather. And why?
For money. You make me sick. As far as I'm concerned, our deal is off. I'm going to tell everybody
what I know. *Everybody!*"

"No you won't," Hugh said coolly and without
hesitation. "Because if you do, I'll make sure your
grandfather stays at Stanford House forever. Then
I'll tell Ms. Tomlinson you broke the rules of your
probation by coming onto my farm and stealing
my property."

Jas inhaled sharply. "How'd you know that?"

"From the surveillance camera I installed. I
have a great shot of you and your boyfriend
sneaking into the barn. By the way, how do you
think *he'll* like the Juvenile Detention Center?"

"No," Jas moaned, knowing she was trapped.
She didn't care about herself, but she couldn't get
Chase in trouble. And Grandfather would die if
he had to stay in the nursing home forever.

"I'm glad you see it my way," said Hugh.

Jas shrank away from him with a feeling of
total defeat.

He's done it again.

But then something inside Jas snapped.

Reaching up, she wrapped her fingers around
the leather reins. She wanted to lash out with the
bridle and swing the metal bit so hard it would
smash into Hugh's face.

"Go ahead, Jas. Do it," he urged, his tone as honeyed as a preacher's. "Because then it really will be over for you. I'll tell the police how once again you attacked me viciously and without provocation," he said, chuckling. "And no matter what you say in your defense, who would ever believe *you*, a convicted criminal?"

No! Jas's fingers tightened around the leather. Violently, she shook her head, wanting to deny what he was saying. But she knew it was over. He'd beaten her for good.

"*I'd* believe her." Miss Hahn's voice rang clear and strong through the small room. Startled, Jas twisted sideways as the door flew open behind her. Pushing past Jas, Miss Hahn strode into the middle of the room, her boots echoing on the wooden floor. She reached up toward the ceiling, made a twisting motion, and the light went on.

Jas blinked, half-blind, seeing Hugh for the first time since the trial. He was dressed impeccably in a long-sleeved riding shirt, ascot, tall black boots, and breeches. He stood ramrod straight, and with the light streaming down on him, Jas saw him for what he was—a ruthless, greedy human.

Her gaze shifted to Miss Hahn.

"You told Hugh I'd be here, didn't you," Jas accused. "You told him everything." Without waiting for a reply, she rushed on, "Only I don't care if you're *both* against me. I know what I need to do."

Boldly, Jas stepped from the shadows. It was time she quit hiding. It was time she told the truth. "I know what Grandfather would want me to do."

Raising her hand, Miss Hahn silenced her. "Don't say anything else, Jas, until Hugh tells us what he's doing here. And why he's threatening you."

Surprised, Jas stared at her. *Wasn't she on Hugh's side?*

Hugh arched one brow. "Threatening her? I don't think so, Diane. In fact, it was the other way around."

"Bull. I heard enough to know what you were trying to do. Jas was smart enough to figure out how you conned the insurance company and now you're trying to keep her quiet. Well, it won't work."

Momentary anger flared in Hugh's eyes, but then his composure returned. "I think you're confused, Diane. And if you persist in taking her side, you'll be sorry."

Miss Hahn's eyes narrowed. Jas had never seen her so angry. And her anger was directed at *Hugh.*

Suddenly, Jas realized that she'd been wrong. *So* wrong. Miss Hahn hadn't been in cahoots with Hugh at all. "Don't threaten me, Robicheaux," Miss Hahn replied, her body shaking with rage. "You forget I've known you for a long time. I'm just sorry I didn't have the guts to confront you twenty years ago when you coolly risked everything–even your friend's life–in order to win."

Hugh humphed. Stretching out one arm at a time, he smoothed the cuffs of his tailored shirt. "It's not too late to take me on, Diane–I even look forward to it. But remember, just like twenty years ago, I'll win." He touched the brim of his cap politely and, without glancing at Jas, strode from the tack room.

Miss Hahn watched him go, then her eyes returned to Jas, and for a second they stared silently at each other.

"Hey, what are you two doing in that tack room?" Chase yelled from outside. "I've got a horse out here that's trying to eat me alive."

"We'll be out in a minute, Chase!" Miss Hahn hollered. "We're having a girl talk."

Sagging against the wall, Jas dropped the grooming box to the floor. Her fingers had been holding the handle so tightly, they were stiff and cramped.

"Thank you," she breathed. "I had no idea..." Her voice trailed off.

"No, thank *you*," Miss Hahn said. Exhaling raggedly, she limped over to a tack trunk and sank down on it. "I had no idea standing up to Hugh would be so hard. And I'm a grown woman. I admire you, Jas. You went after him, and you've got a lot less years than I do."

Jas shook her head. "Sure, I went after him. But it's too late. I lost."

"You *didn't* lose. You have other people on your side now. Dr. Danvers and I will help you get Hugh."

Jas's eyes widened with surprise. "All this time I thought you were on Hugh's side. How do you know what's going on? How do you know about Shadow?"

"The day I saw you jumping Shadow, I knew the horse looked familiar. Dr. Danvers had already mentioned your—and his—suspicions about Whirlwind's death. Then he told me about your suspicions about Shadow.

"Today, when we arrived at Lydia's, you and Chase were so gloomy, I knew something was up. I cornered Chase and he told me about Dr. Danvers's phone call confirming that Shadow and Aladdin were the same horse. Chase also told me you believed I was in cahoots with

Hugh—though I should have guessed by the way you acted around me." Glancing down, Miss Hahn massaged her knee as if it hurt. "I just thought you hated being at the farm, and that after your experience, you didn't want to trust anyone."

"At first I did hate being at the farm," Jas admitted. "And I hated being a foster kid. It wasn't until today that I realized that I kind of think of the farm as home now," she added. Embarrassed, Jas rushed on, "You could have helped me if I had trusted you. I'm so sorry. Still, Chase *wasn't* supposed to tell you."

"But I'm glad he did," Miss Hahn said. "I was coming in to talk when I found you with Hugh. I have no idea how he knew you were going to be here today—I'd hate to think Lydia had anything to do with it."

"She wouldn't be the first to succumb to Hugh. Besides, as horrible as it was, I'm glad I talked to him, because now I know that Whirlwind's alive!"

"Whirlwind's alive?"

Jas nodded excitedly. "Hugh killed a ringer, just like he did with Aladdin. That means—"

"Jas," Miss Hahn cut her off. "Don't get your hopes up. If the insurance company goes after Hugh, the first thing he'll do is hire the best lawyer in the state. He'll never admit to anything, which means we'll never find out what happened to Whirlwind."

"But-t-t..." Jas stammered. She stared at Miss Hahn, not wanting to believe what she was saying, even though she knew it was true. If Hugh was cornered, he'd never admit to his scam. She was lucky enough to find out that Whirlwind was alive.

"At least I know she's not dead," Jas finally said, her tone resigned. "And I can always hope that she's being well cared for and loved."

"Maybe we won't find her, Jas, but I promise we'll get Hugh," Miss Hahn said. "Mr. Jenkins, the president of the insurance company, is one of Second Chance Farm's main supporters. He's going to be very interested in hearing that Hugh might have cheated his company."

"But Hugh said a clerk was mistaken about the identification numbers."

"Forget what Hugh said. He's been twisting people around all his life, and it's time someone stopped him."

Jas frowned. "You sound like you know him well."

"I do," Miss Hahn said as she patted herself on the knee. "It's a long story that I'll tell you all about when we have time. But right now, there's a horse waiting for you." Miss Hahn slid a saddle onto her arms. "Come on. I'll help you tack the big guy up."

Jas hesitated when Miss Hahn left the tack room. *Should I tell her she shouldn't get rid of Shadow?*

But Jas knew that when she and Grandfather moved to an apartment, it would be hard enough to make ends meet. She knew she would have to get a job after school. She knew she wouldn't have time for a talented but demanding horse.

Bending slowly, Jas picked up the grooming box. With a heavy heart, she followed Miss Hahn out the door.

Chapter 24

"All right, big guy," Jas said as she patted Shadow's neck. "Let's show Lydia what you can do."

Eyes focused on the first jump, Jas steered Shadow down the line of fences. He sailed over a three-foot-six fence and then a low spread as if they were not even there. Turning Shadow down the center, Jas bounced him through a tight in and out, then circled right and jumped the last line of fences smoothly.

When she slowed him to a trot, Jas felt like bursting. "You were great," she exclaimed as her fingers dug into his mane. Although she never wanted to let go, she knew she had to.

Standing by the gate, Lydia and Miss Hahn clapped their approval.

"I love him!" Lydia exclaimed. "I can't believe you got him from some killer auction, Diane."

"All the credit goes to Jas," Miss Hahn said. "She's the one who discovered him."

Jas flushed. Steering Shadow away from the gate, she loosened the reins and let him stretch out into an easy walk to cool off.

Chase vaulted over the fence. He jogged over, and when he fell in step beside Shadow, he gave Jas a funny look. "I thought you were going to knock down all the fences?"

"I changed my mind. Shadow deserves the best, and Lydia can give it to him."

"But you two are a perfect team," Chase protested. "You're the one who can take him to the top."

Halting Shadow, Jas smiled down at him. "Hey, whatever happened to the person who believed a horse didn't have to jump a fence or win a race to be worth something?"

He shrugged. "Okay, so I've reconsidered. Shadow loves jumping so much that I think he'd be miserable just hanging around a pasture."

"You're right. He would," Jas said as she pulled off her helmet and threw it to him. Swinging her leg over the cantle, she dismounted, sliding the last few feet to the ground. Chase gently caught her around the waist. Her heart skipped a beat.

"You know Lydia really likes him," he said as his breath rustled her hair.

She nodded.

"And you're okay with it?"

"Just okay. So drop it, all right?"

"All right." He let go of her waist. Pulling the reins over Shadow's head, Jas ran up his stirrups, then led him out the gate.

Lydia watched as they approached. Jas took a deep breath, knowing that she had to get it over with.

"He's everything I want in a horse, Diane," Lydia gushed. "Bold, athletic, handsome, sane. When can I have him?"

"I'm sorry, Lydia," Miss Hahn said. "I'm afraid I can't let you have this one. I've changed my mind."

"What do you mean, you changed your mind?" Lydia gasped.

"What do you mean, you changed your mind?" Jas repeated in confused excitement.

Miss Hahn gave Jas a long, thoughtful stare. Then she turned back to face Lydia. "Shadow belongs to Jas. She's the one who found him. She's the one who recognized his potential, and–" her voice broke with emotion. "She's the one who really loves him."

Jas's mouth fell open. "But I won't be able..."

"We'll figure something out," Miss Hahn said firmly. "I promise."

"Yes!" Chase yelled as he punched the air with his fists.

Lydia put her hands on her hips. "But when

you brought the horse over, you implied that if I was interested, I could adopt him," she said, sounding as imperious as Hugh. "I'll even throw in a big contribution to the farm. How's that sound?"

Miss Hahn's nostrils flared. "I never promised you this horse, Lydia. I'm sorry if you misunderstood me."

"Well, then." Fuming and at a loss for words, Lydia stalked off.

"Sore loser," Chase muttered under his breath.

"She'll get over it," Miss Hahn said. "She's just jealous because she knows that Shadow and Jas have what it takes to be champions."

Chase grinned proudly. "That's what I just said to Jas."

Jas was still frozen to the spot, her lips parted in disbelief. She was afraid to say anything for fear she'd misunderstood. "But we already talked about how I won't have the time or the money to take care of Shadow."

"I said we'd figure out something," Miss Hahn repeated, a stubborn look in her eyes. "*I'll* figure out something. In fact, I've been mulling over an idea already."

Snorting, Shadow butted Jas with his nose as if he were tired of being ignored. Jas turned and flung her arms around his neck. "Don't worry, no one's forgotten about you."

"So what's your idea?" Chase asked impatiently.

Miss Hahn tapped her lip. "Now, it's just an idea, and I haven't thought it all through, but...how would you and your grandfather like to live at the farm?"

Jas's brows shot up. "What?"

"I don't mean in the house with me," Miss Hahn explained quickly. "I'd get someone to donate a house trailer. The place desperately needs a caretaker. The volunteers can do only so much, and when Chase goes back to school this fall I'll be overwhelmed. I know how handy your grandfather is, and of course I know what a hard worker you are."

"Yee-hah!" Chase whooped. "I think that's a terrific idea."

"Are you serious?" Jas couldn't believe her ears. Miss Hahn's idea sounded too good to be true. "I mean, I don't know how strong Grandfather will be, and I have to go back to school at the end of August, too."

"The things I need your grandfather to take care of won't require a lot of strength. *Something's* breaking in that madhouse every day." Miss Hahn's voice rose in excitement. "And having another responsible person living at the farm means that I could leave once in a while. Maybe even go to a few horse shows."

"Yes!" Jas screamed deliriously. "I think your idea is wonderful! And I think Grandfather will love it, too. Thank you, Miss Hahn! Thank you!" she exclaimed, throwing her arms around Miss Hahn.

Snorting in fear, Shadow threw up his head, jerking the reins from Jas's hand. With a shake of his mane, he trotted off, the reins dangling.

"Oh, no!" Jas gasped, taking off after him.

Breaking into a canter, he headed for the other side of the barn. Jas realized where he was going–straight for Lydia's cow pasture.

"Shadow!" she cried. "Whoa!"

Ignoring her, he cantered right for the four-board fence. After nickering a greeting, Shadow jumped into the pasture.

Jas slid to a halt, Miss Hahn and Chase stopping beside her. She groaned as she watched Shadow gallop toward the cows.

"He's going to catch his leg in the reins and break it," she moaned.

"Or run a cow through the fence," Chase added.

With a sigh, Jas turned toward Miss Hahn. "Are you sure you still like your idea? Grandfather, Shadow, and I might be more trouble than we're worth."

"You'll be worth it." Miss Hahn patted her shoulder. "I'm sure."

Chase grinned at the two of them. "I like the idea, too. I like it a *lot*. But now we better catch that crazy horse. Jas, you stay here and keep an eye on him. I'll get his halter."

"And I'll get the bucket of grain," Miss Hahn offered.

Jas nodded, too choked up to speak. Walking over to the fence, she propped her arms on the top board and watched Shadow prance through the herd. He looked like a wild stallion, his tail streaming behind him as he scattered the cows across the green pasture.

Jas smiled, happier than she'd ever been. She knew this was only the beginning. Even with Miss Hahn and Danvers on her side, going after Hugh was going to be tough. But she welcomed the challenge.

Her court hearing was also fast approaching. The thought of facing the judge made Jas's mouth go dry. But at least this time she wouldn't be alone. Chase, Miss Hahn, and Grandfather would be there to help her get through it all.

After that, she and Grandfather could finally settle into their new life at Second Chance Farm.

Then she could start the search for Whirlwind.